Off-beat audience

with a crime king...

Hutch turned to the cedar bench facing the racketeer, spread his towel and sat down. Starsky spread
his to his partner's left and sat also. . . .

"Someone," Tallman said, "who envies me is attempting to frame me with your murders."

Starsky said, "We haven't been murdered yet, so
you're in the clear."

"I know, but they'll try again. Sometime today or
tomorrow, or tomorrow night. No later. If they
kill you after that, I'll have no motive, and they
can't frame me. That's really what this is
about . . ."

STARSKY & HUTCH

adapted by Max Franklin

**TV'S TOUGHEST TWOSOME GANG UP
ON THE UNDERWORLD IN A
NONSTOP ADVENTURE NOVEL**

Now a new BBC TV Series
STARSKY & HUTCH

Starring David Soul and Paul Michael Glaser
Created and Written by
William Blinn

A Spelling–Goldberg Production

Watch for the next adventure of

STARSKY & HUTCH:
"Kill Huggy Bear"

Published by Ballantine Books

Starsky
&
Hutch

Created and Written by
William Blinn

Adapted by
Max Franklin

Now a new BBC TV Series
Starring David Soul
and Paul Michael Glaser

A Spelling—Goldberg Production

BALLANTINE BOOKS • NEW YORK

Library of Congress Catalog Card Number: 75-38993

ISBN 0-345-24996-8-150

Manufactured in the United States of America

First Edition: February 1976
Second Printing: June 1976

First Special Printing: March 1976

Chapter 1

As THE BUS hissed to a stop at Fifth and Hill streets, the young man in patched Levis, blue sport shirt, and blue sneakers was the first one off. Swinging down to the sidewalk with athletic grace, he strode northward along Hill toward Fourth Street on the opposite side of the street from the Public Library.

The block-square grounds of the Public Library extended to the southwest corner of Fourth and Hill. The other three corners were occupied by pay parking lots. Despite the posted charge of $2.25 for all-day parking, all three lots were full.

The young man paused on the sidewalk to run his gaze over the cars on the southeast lot. When he saw nothing to interest him, he crossed the street to check the other two lots. After studying the cars parked in both of them, he made a disgusted face and headed back along Hill toward Fifth again.

At Fifth he turned left and walked down the steep hill to Pershing Square. Crossing the street, he headed along the edge of the park to the small, glass-enclosed building housing the escalators to the parking garage beneath the park.

As he took a down escalator, he muttered to himself, "Sonovabitch wants a miracle. Never find a thing like that in a million years."

1

He continued all the way down to the lowest level. After making a complete tour of it, he walked up the ramp to the next level.

At the top level of the garage he finally found what he was looking for. It would have been hard to miss. It was a bright red Torino with a foot-wide white stripe running across the roof just forward of the rear window, down the sides, and then forward, tapering to points at the hood.

An expression of mixed surprise and pleasure formed on the young man's face. Glancing around and seeing no one nearby, he went over to the driver's side to try the door. He wasn't surprised to find it locked. After peering through the glass at the opposite door and seeing that the lock button was pressed down, he took a thin piece of spring steel from his pocket and inserted it in the door lock. It took him approximately thirty seconds to get the door open.

Sliding into the front seat, he tried the glove compartment and found it unlocked. He poked through the various papers in the compartment until he found the registration certificate enclosed in a plastic holder. The car was registered to a Terrance Crowder with an address in the Boyle Heights district of Los Angeles.

Taking a scrap of paper and a pencil stub from his shirt pocket, the young man copied down the name and address of the car owner. Then he replaced the registration certificate in the glove compartment, climbed from the car, and used his picklock to relock the car door.

As he took the escalator up to street level, he started whistling.

The little café was on Hilgard Avenue, directly across from the UCLA campus. It was crowded with students, some eating sandwiches or ice cream confections, but most merely sipping Cokes or coffee.

A pretty blond girl sat alone in the rearmost booth, a Coke glass with nothing remaining in it but melting ice on the table before her, concentrating on an open book. About nineteen, she wore a plain beige knit suit which probably would have looked conservative on most girls, but which she somehow managed to look daring in. Perhaps it was because it was just tight enough to cling to her excellent figure in an almost lascivious manner, making her seem ripe and sensual.

She grew conscious of someone stopping beside her booth, but was too engrossed in her book to look up until a male voice said, "Hey, aren't you Patty Talbot?"

The questioner was about twenty-two, with a rather good-looking face and dark, shoulder-length hair. He was dressed in worn Levis and a sport shirt. The girl wasn't particularly drawn to hippie types, but she was turned on by virility, and the young man seemed to exude it. He had the lean, muscular, athletic build that she particularly liked in a man.

"Yes," she said, with a touch more warmth than mere politeness would have required.

"Stan Cather," he said. "We met over at the Student Union couple of weeks ago. Jerry Taylor introduced us."

The name Jerry Taylor meant nothing to Patty, and she was sure she would not have forgotten a man with a build like his. Not a stupid girl, she instantly divined that he had merely found out her name from someone in the café, and was making a pickup attempt. But she had no objection to being picked up by this particular man.

"Oh, yes," she said, smiling. "Good old Jerry."

He looked vaguely surprised, leading her to the conclusion that he wasn't quite as bright as he appeared at first glance. "Buy you a refill?" he asked, nodding toward her glass.

"If you'd like."

There was no booth service. Picking up her glass, he carried it over to the counter and ordered another Coke for her and a cup of coffee for himself. She resumed reading her book until he returned. But as he set down the glass and cup and slid into the seat opposite her, she closed the book and shoved it aside.

Reading the title, *Principles of Western Law,* upside down, he said, "Sounds deep. Law school?"

"Pre-law," she said. "What are you?"

He hiked his eyebrows. "Male, single, twenty-two. What am I what?"

"In school, I mean."

"Oh. I'm not in school."

She creased her forehead. "Then why were you at the Student Union the day we met?" After a pause, she added sardonically, "If you were."

"There on business," he said.

"Oh? What business?"

Pursing his lips, he considered her in silence for a time, started to say something, and instead took a sip of his coffee.

"Top secret?" she inquired. "Let me guess. You're an FBI informer trying to work your way into some radical student group like the college-level YMCA."

Grinning, he shook his head. "Hundred and eighty degrees out of phase."

"Mean you're a radical trying to work your way into the FBI?"

His grin widened, and again he shook his head.

"What, then?"

After considering her with pursed lips, he said, "I don't know enough about you to tell you just yet."

"How much would you have to know?"

He took another sip of coffee while he rolled that around in his mind. Finally he said, "Let's start with how you feel about grass."

She took a thoughtful sip of her Coke, examining him over the rim of the glass. "You a nark?"

"God no!" he said with a pained expression. "This time you're really a hundred and eighty degrees off."

Her face registered enlightenment. "You're a dealer! You were in the Student Union because you were peddling."

Glancing around, he made a cautioning motion. "You haven't answered my question. What's your attitude toward pot?"

"Love it. Signed a petition to get it legalized."

He smiled at her. "Then you wouldn't turn in a dealer?"

"Aw, come on, love. I might shake him down for a joint, but I wouldn't snitch." She looked at him expectantly.

"Not in here," he said. "They've got a tough rule."

"I wasn't planning to light up. Just to stick it in my purse."

"I only give out free samples on dates," he told her. "Maybe if we go out on a date sometime."

"Like when?" she inquired.

"Like tonight?"

After briefly considering, she said, "I have to study for a test, but I could make it later."

"How later?"

"Ten-thirty, maybe?"

"Date," he said. "Where?"

"I live in the General Dorm. Know where it is?"

He nodded. "Room number?"

"You won't need it, because I'll meet you in the lobby. But it's two-twelve."

"That's easy to remember," he said. "Temperature of boiling water." He glanced over at a wall clock. "Got to split now, honey. Have things to do before tonight."

He slid from the booth. Looking up at him, she asked, "Any particular way I should dress?"

"Anything appropriate for a walk on the beach. I'm wearing what I got on."

"Oh, we're going for a walk on the beach?"

"Where better to puff grass?" he inquired.

She nodded. "Yeah, I guess. Okay, ten-thirty, and I'll be in slacks and flat shoes."

Elevating one hand, palm out, in a gesture of good-bye, he walked out.

He had to walk clear to Wilshire Boulevard to catch a bus, a distance of several blocks. While still half a block from his bus stop, but in sight of it, he saw a bus just pulling away. Since it would be twenty minutes before another came along, he decided to make a phone call.

He found an outside phone near the bus stop. He dropped in a coin, dialed a number, and asked a voice at the other end for an extension.

When there was an answer on the extension, he said, "Stan Cather. All set for tonight. . . . No, I won't have any trouble getting her there. It's already set that we're taking a walk on the beach. . . . I figure about midnight, half-hour one way or the other. I'm picking her up at ten-thirty."

There was another pause, then, "Because she has to study for a test. Let me get this straight, now. All I got to do is get her stoned and start to lay her, and then these fake cops will shine the light and pretend to write us up for public indecency. They're not gonna hassle us too much, are they? . . . Then I'm off the hook?"

After a final pause he said, "Roger," and hung up.

At five P.M. Stan Cather left his room on Franklin Street in Hollywood and caught a bus to the Boyle Heights district. It was a four-block walk from the bus stop to the address he had copied down from the car registration for the red and white Torino.

The car owner seemed to be home from wherever in downtown Los Angeles he worked, because the Torino was in a carport attached to the house. After a casual glance around to make sure he was unobserved, Cather strolled into the carport, lifted the hood, and used a screwdriver to make a small adjustment. Pushing the hood closed again as quietly as possible, he strolled out of the carport and up the street.

He now didn't have to worry about the car owner lousing up his plans by using the car that evening. Without a readjustment, there was no way the car could be started, even with a battery jumper. Of course, an expert mechanic could eventually find the trouble, but mechanics weren't easily available evenings. The probability was that if the owner did plan to use the Torino, he would give up after a little tinkering, decide to phone a repair garage in the morning, and arrange for other transportation that night.

Cather found a restaurant with reasonable prices, had some dinner, then killed time in a tavern until nine-thirty. When he returned to the home of the Torino owner, the car was still in the carport and the drapes of the house were drawn.

He made the necessary readjustment, unlocked both the car door and the ignition-steering-wheel lock with his picklock, rolled the car backward into the street, started the engine, and drove off.

7

Chapter 2

THE DARK SEDAN was parked on a bluff overlooking the Coast Highway north of Santa Monica. It was pulled off on the grassy shoulder of a narrow road that wound down from the bluff top to the highway, a spot which gave the occupants of the car a clear view of the highway for a half-mile in both directions.

There were two men in the car, both in their mid-forties. The driver was tall and angular, with a long, sharp-boned face and a hook nose. The man in the front seat next to him had the square, powerful build of a Japanese wrestler, but that was the only thing Oriental about him. His hair was light blond, his skin almost albino white, and his thick features had a Slavic look.

Although it was a few minutes past midnight, visibility was excellent because of a bright full moon. Only a typical mid-May fog beginning to creep in from the ocean threatened.

The bony driver said worriedly, "Fog keeps rolling in, won't be able to spot the damn thing."

"Should be here before it gets that thick," his burly companion assured him.

The driver lifted a thermos bottle from the seat between them and poured himself a cup of coffee. After one sip, he said, "Jesus, did you sugar this too?"

"Too? Did you?"

"Christ," the driver said disgustedly. "I told you I was fixing it." He emptied the cup out the window and screwed the lid back onto the thermos bottle.

"Sugar's good for you this time of night," the burly man said. "Gives you extra energy."

Unscrewing the cap again, he poured himself a cup. Tasting it, he smacked his lips.

"Jesus," the bony man said. "You can drink that, you'll drink anything."

There was silence for some minutes. The burly man finished his coffee and put the lid back on the thermos bottle. The driver looked at the luminous dial of his watch.

"Hope they get here pretty soon," he said. "I want to be in the place by one o'clock."

"Why one o'clock?" the squarely built man asked.

"Movie on the tube I never saw the end of. *Red River*. John Wayne."

"You never saw the end?"

"No." The thin man added quickly, "But don't tell me."

"What's to tell?" the burly man asked. "He wins. He always wins. Besides, it's on tomorrow afternoon, too."

Headlights appeared from the south, and both men peered in that direction. They relaxed when a Volkswagen went by, but immediately straightened in their seats again when a second pair of headlights appeared from the same direction. This time, as the car neared, they could make out its red color in the bright moonlight and the wide white stripe running horizontally across the rear part of its roof and along its sides.

"That's the one," the burly man said.

"Yeah," the driver agreed.

He started the engine, put the car in gear, and without lights started down the winding road to the highway below. As he turned onto it, he flicked on his lights. He speeded up until they spotted the tail-lights of the red and white Torino about a hundred yards ahead of them, then slowed down and maintained the same distance between them.

In the Torino a tape deck was playing rock music. Patty Talbot, in slacks and a man's flannel shirt, leaned back with her eyes closed and a dreamy expression on her face, thoroughly enjoying the music. Stan Cather drove carefully, neither too slow nor too fast, the only sensible way to drive a stolen car.

After a time he slowed down, swung left across the highway onto a narrow gravel road, and followed it a short distance to a deserted beach. A narrow band of scrubby grass edged the beach, pushing up through ground that was half dirt and half sand. From previous experience Cather knew that he would mire down if he drove onto the sand beach, but that the ground where the grass grew was firm enough to support car wheels. He drove along the band of grass about twenty yards from the gravel road before parking.

When he cut the lights and the engine, the music abruptly stopped.

Opening her eyes and sitting up, Patty said, "Hey, why'd you turn off the tape?"

Taking a packet of cigarette papers and a small tobacco sack from his pocket, Cather began to roll a marijuana cigarette. "Didn't do anything to the tape," he said. "Motor shuts off, the tape shuts off."

"Well, turn the motor on then. That's my favorite group."

He stopped rolling the cigarette long enough to turn on the ignition so that the tape player could run off the battery. As the music started up again, he said, "Happy now?"

Watching him resume rolling the cigarette, she said, "I'll be happier when I get a hit off that joint."

He licked the edges together and twisted the end. As he put it into his mouth and dug a paper of matches from his pocket, he asked, "How's it hit you back?"

"I really groove on good stuff," she said. "Makes me all warm and inhibitionless. Get agreeable to most anything."

"Hmm," he said with interest. "This is good stuff. Not what I deal, but what I save for friends. Real hashish."

He lit the joint, tossed the match out the window, then rolled up the window. He inhaled a deep drag, held it, and passed the joint to her. As she started to drag, he frowned at the open window on her side and released the smoke from his lungs.

"Roll up your window," he said.

Glancing at him sideways, she made no immediate answer because she was holding down inhaled smoke. Passing back the joint, she finally exhaled and said, "Why? It's a super night out."

"Because it gets better the more smoke we can keep inside. It's like a steam bath for heads."

She smiled at him in the darkness. "That's far out. That really is." She rolled up the window. "But what about that walk on the beach?"

"After the smoke, after the almost anything you mentioned." He took a drag and passed the joint back.

"Don't talk so dirty in front of a lady," she said, but she was smiling at him provocatively as she took another drag.

The dark sedan had also slowed and turned left onto the gravel road, but the driver cut the lights as he turned. Only a few yards along the road he pulled over onto the grassy shoulder and cut the engine. Both men watched as the Torino drove a few yards along the edge of the beach, stopped, and cut its headlights. Then they reached into the back seat for two black leather cases about the size and shape of clarinet cases. Laying them on their laps, they lifted out twin double-barreled ten-gauge sawed-off shotguns. Closing the cases again and sliding them from their laps onto the seat between them, they broke the guns to check that both barrels were loaded, then snapped them shut again.

Getting out of the car, they walked in single file along the edge of the gravel road, the sawed-off shotguns held muzzle downward alongside their legs, the burly man in the lead. When they reached the band of scrubby grass edging the beach, the burly man continued on out onto the sand for a few paces in order to approach the car on the driver's side. The thin man walked along the band of grass to approach it on the right side.

As they neared the car, they could hear music coming from it. They made no effort to walk cautiously, but they made no noise, either. Unhurriedly they approached from either side, and simultaneously bent to peer into the car. They could see nothing through the cloud of smoke inside.

Straightening, the men looked across the top of the car roof at each other. In a low but conversational voice the burly man said, "Smoking that stuff's against the law, ain't it?"

Equally low, and equally conversationally, the thin man said, "Yeah. Want to stop 'em?"

"It's what John Wayne would do," the burly man said.

There was no indication from inside the car that the occupants had either heard them or seen them, which was not surprising in view of the volume of the music and the density of the smoke.

In unison the two men moved around in front of

the car, so as not to hit each other in their own cross-fire. Resting their elbows on the hood, they aimed the shotguns at the windshield, nodded to each other, and fired all four barrels at once.

The guns were loaded with magnum shells of 00 buckshot, which made for a tremendous explosion and tremendous damage. The windshield literally disap-peared, the charge ripped through the interior and took out the back window.

The two men took the time to peer in at the mangled bodies in the front seat. Then they started back toward their own car, not unhurriedly now, but loping with their guns held at high port. Sliding into the front seat from either side of the car, they slammed closed the doors. The thin man dropped his gun into his partner's lap, started the engine, made a tight U-turn, and drove back to the highway. Turning south, he drove a good fifty yards before switching on his headlights.

Meantime the burly man was packing both guns back into their leather cases. When he finished, he set them on the floor of the back seat.

Glancing at his luminous wrist watch, the driver said in a disgusted tone, "I don't think we're going to make it."

"Make what?" the burly man asked with a touch of alarm, swinging around in his seat to peer through the rear window.

"The end of John Wayne in *Red River*."

The burly man exhaled his held breath. "Jesus, make yourself a little clearer, will you?" he said in a querulous voice. "I thought we had cops on our tail."

Chapter 3

THE GIRL DRIVING the red and white Torino south on Figueroa Street was in her early twenties. Blond, deeply tanned, and busty, she wore a white long-sleeved wool sweater against the early morning chill, but apparently her long, shapely legs were immune to cold, because they were bare to the edges of her skimpy white shorts. Her feet were all but bare, too, her sandals consisting of nothing but soles, small leather loops through which her big toes were thrust, and narrow thongs looped behind her heels.

In the front seat next to her, slumped forward with his knees pressed against the dashboard and his head resting against the back of the seat, was Detective Dave Starsky. A leanly muscled man in his late twenties, about five feet eleven, he had dark brown, rather bushy hair and blue eyes. He was dressed in faded Levis, a T-shirt, a dark blue windbreaker about ready for the Goodwill truck, and a knitted Los Angeles Rams warmup cap. Despite his relaxed position and his slitted eyes, he gave an impression of constant alertness, as though he really missed nothing going on around him and, if necessary, he could bounce from repose into instant action.

As they passed Third Street, Starsky said, "Next block on the right."

Shooting him a sideways glance, she said, "Thought you were asleep."

Straightening in his seat and smiling at her, he said, "Cops never sleep. Ever on the alert to guard you defenseless citizens from the predators who roam the dark byways of the city jungle. Particularly defenseless young girls."

"Who guards defenseless young girls from predatory, sweet-talking cops?"

"Their innate virtue, Cindy. Their innate virtue. Parking lot on the right."

The indicated lot was just beyond a small, square, one-story building with a sign on its front reading VINNIE'S GYM. The girl swung the Torino onto the lot and parked next to the only other car there, a brown, rather beat-up two-year-old Ford sedan.

Reaching over, Starsky turned off the ignition and pocketed the keys. The girl examined him with a mixture of fondness and exasperation.

"You know, after the kind of night we spent, a lot of guys would at least give me a ride to my apartment."

"You're right, Cindy," Starsky agreed. "But I'd be late to work if I did."

"It's ten minutes from here."

He nodded. "Ten minutes from here to your place, then forty-five minutes inside your place. I know how it is with us, sweetness."

Her expression suggested she didn't know whether to be flattered or incensed. She settled for resignation. Leaning across, she gave him a solid kiss on the mouth. When she straightened again, he eyed her contemplatively, as though reconsidering driving her home after all. Then he gave his head a regretful shake.

"You're a beast, you know," she said, lifting her purse from the seat between them and getting out of the car.

Picking up a brown paper bag lying at his feet,

Starsky got out the other side. They looked at each other across the roof of the car, then he nodded toward the corner across the street.

"Bus stop's over there," he said.

"I know," she said, continuing to look at him.

"Mad?"

"Yes."

Smiling, he said, "Good. It'll give us something to talk about tomorrow night."

Giving her a good-bye wink, he turned toward a side entrance to the gymnasium. She watched until he disappeared inside, her expression again a mixture of fondness and exasperation, then shook her head in wonder at her own forbearance, turned, and headed for the bus stop.

Since it was not yet eight in the morning, there was only one patron in the gymnasium. Detective Kenneth Hutchinson, wearing nothing but gym shorts and sneakers, lay on his back on a weight bench, rhythmically pushing a barbell upward to arms' length, then lowering it to his chest again.

Hutchinson was also in his late twenties, had blue eyes, and had the same leanly muscled build as Starsky. But there the resemblance stopped. About two inches taller than Starsky's five feet eleven, he had blond hair and a sort of genteel handsomeness. Even working out in gym attire, he gave an impression of what Bostonians call "breeding." Just as Starsky was obviously a product of the streets, Hutch Hutchinson obviously came from a cultured background.

Starsky seated himself on a bench a short distance to one side of the weight bench. Although aware of his presence, Hutch said nothing for a few moments, merely continuing his presses.

Eventually, without slowing the rhythm of his exercise, the blond detective said, "You're late."

Starsky shrugged. "Don't want to hurt your feelings,

but coming down here to watch you sweat is not the high point of my day." He opened the paper bag on his lap. "I got coffee and Danish. Want to share?"

Making a face, Hutch said, "Do I ever?"

"No, but I keep hoping."

Starsky drew a lidded Styrofoam cup from the bag, set it on the bench next to him, took a paper napkin from the bag to spread next to him on the other side, and laid a large Danish sweet roll on the napkin. Carefully folding the paper bag, he laid it on the bench as well.

Hutch placed the barbell on the rack, sat up, and mopped his perspiring face with a towel. He gazed with disapproval at the sweet roll.

Coming to his feet, Hutch started toward a door at the rear of the gym that had large black lettering on it reading LOCKER ROOM—SHOWERS. Over his shoulder he said, "Let me catch a shower, I'll be ready to go."

A man in his mid-fifties, hard-bodied, in perfect physical shape, came from the locker room door as Hutch neared it. He was wearing slacks, a T-shirt, and sneakers, and carried in his arms a large pile of freshly laundered towels. He and Hutch passed without speaking, and Hutch disappeared through the locker-room door. As the man went past Starsky en route to a laundry bin next to the front counter, he threw a disapproving look at the coffee cup and sweet roll on the bench.

"Morning, Vinnie," Starsky said. He uncapped the coffee cup.

"Shouldn't drink that crap," Vinnie said. "It'll eat your gut away."

Holding the cup in his left hand, clasping his right to his heart, Starsky said, "Mama, I met a doctor. I think he loves me." He took a sip of his coffee.

In the act of loading the towels into the laundry

bin, Vinnie said without turning around, "Funny, funny. You're a big comedian, right?"

"No, not a comedian," Starsky said brightly. "Try again, Vinnie." Setting down the coffee cup, he picked up the sweet roll and took a bite of it.

Closing the laundry bin lid, Vinnie emitted a snort indicating total lack of interest in what Starsky was or was not. He started back toward the locker room.

As he passed Starsky again, the detective said, "Don't you ever get curious, Vinnie? About what me and Hutch do for a living?"

Halting a few feet beyond, the man slowly turned around. In an emphatic tone obviously meant to make clear that he minded his own business, he said, "I got no questions."

"Keeping your head in the sand, huh?" Starsky said, enjoying himself.

"Better my head in the sand than my ass in a sling. You know what you're doing, that's enough for me."

Hutch had left the door to the locker room open. His voice called, "Yeah, Starsky and I know what we're doing, Vinnie."

The gym proprietor turned in Hutchinson's direction. Hutch's head poked around the corner. His hair was wet and there was a towel over his shoulders.

Grinning, he said, "But damned if we know *why* we're doing it."

His head disappeared again. Vinnie continued on in toward the locker room. Starsky took another bite of his sweet roll.

Starsky had finished his breakfast and had disposed of the cup, paper bag, and napkin in a trash can by the time Hutch came from the shower room. The blond detective was dressed in well-pressed slacks, a turtleneck sweater, and a tan checked sport coat. He

19

looked like a model for a *Playboy* article on men's attire.

As the pair emerged from the side entrance of the gym, Starsky nodded toward the two cars parked side by side and asked, "Yours or mine?"

"Mine," Hutch said. "That suspension of yours makes the thing ride like a rock on a washboard."

Shrugging, Starsky said agreeably, "Okay."

Hutch unlocked the brown Ford, climbed under the wheel, and reached across to pull up the button of the other door. As Starsky got in, Hutch pulled down a small clipboard from the sun visor and rested it on the steering wheel. He began reading aloud from a check list.

"Glove compartment."

Opening the glove compartment and peering into it, Starsky said, "Shells. Your Beretta. My thirty-eight. Flares. Tear gas grenades, four."

"Shotgun," Hutch read.

Leaning forward and beneath his seat, Starsky pulled out a rack that slid in and out on rollers, like a drawer. It contained a number of items. Starsky pushed open the slide bolt of a riot gun just far enough to see that there was a shell in the chamber.

"Shotgun racked and loaded," he said.

"Radios?"

"Two," Starsky said, touching them. "Fresh batteries in the case."

"Flashlight?"

"Here," Starsky said, touching it.

"And the book," Hutch finished.

He replaced the clipboard over the visor. Starsky slid the rack back beneath his seat, reached up under the dashboard, and brought out a thick notebook anchored to a chain. Opening it, he riffled through the wanted posters and police bulletins it contained. "Nothing real new or real hot," he said.

Hutch started the engine. Putting the book back under the dashboard, Starsky reached just left of it and drew out a radio microphone. He pressed the transmit button as Hutch backed up the car.

"Cruiser Three to Control One. Come in, Control One."

Hutch shifted into drive and drove off the lot, turning right. From the radio speaker came "Control One to Cruiser Three. Go ahead."

"Cruiser Three here," Starsky said. "Log us on the street and rolling." He looked at his watch. "The time, eight hundred hours."

"You're logged in at eight hundred hours," the radio voice confirmed. "Good hunting, Cruiser Three."

Starsky hung up the mike on its hook beneath the dashboard. The car drifted along, Hutch driving slowly, his eyes missing nothing on the left side of the street, Starsky equally attentive to everything happening on the right side. They cruised up one street and down another of the downtown area, randomly, yet in a pattern which eventually would cover the whole area.

After a time Hutch asked, "How'd it go with Cindy?"

Without taking his gaze from the passing parade, Starsky said, "Acceptable, acceptable. You still seeing what's-her-name?"

"Still seeing what's-her-name," Hutch acknowledged. "Took her to whatchamacallit and asked her to wear my thingamajig."

Grinning, but not looking around, Starsky said, "Didn't know it was that serious."

"It's not," Hutch said—then, with sudden urgency, "But *that* might be."

Starsky swung around to follow his partner's gaze. On the opposite side of the street they were approaching a group of early morning commuters waiting for a bus. At the rear of the group stood a thin little man in a wrinkled suit. He was rather nondescript, nearing sixty with a forgettable face. It was not the face that had attracted Hutch's attention, but the man's furtive manner. Like the others, he was peering down the street in the direction of the anticipated bus, but only at brief intervals. His attention kept sliding to the well-dressed man standing directly in front of him.

"Dip?" Starsky said.

"Looks like," Hutch said, still frowning in the little man's direction as they cruised past the corner. "Familiar too."

"Yeah," Starsky said, peering back over his shoulder. "That's a face a mother might forget, but I can't seem to."

Reaching up underneath the dashboard, he pulled out the book and began leafing through mug shots.

Lifting his right hand from the wheel, Hutch snapped his fingers. "Coley? Thought he was in the Place. Three to five."

Starsky stopped flipping pages to look down at front and profile photographs of the man they had seen standing on the corner. "*Was* is the word. Paroled two months ago."

They had come to the next intersection. Hutch started to make a U-turn, but had to wait for traffic.

"What a record!" Starsky said with something akin to admiration, his gaze still fixed on the make sheet. "Been in every jail in the state except debtors' prison, and only missed that because it was abolished."

Traffic eased enough for Hutch to complete the U-turn. Starsky closed the book and put it away. As they drifted by the corner again, this time on the same side of the street, Starsky closely examined the man from the corner of his eye without appearing to look at him.

"That's Coley for sure," he said in a positive tone.

There was a parking place just beyond the bus loading zone. Hutch pulled into it.

Chapter 4

WITH THE THIN man's attention divided between an approaching bus a couple of blocks away and the well-dressed man in front of him, he was unaware of the two detectives alighting from the brown Ford and moving in behind him. He waited until the bus crossed the next intersection and began to pull in at the bus stop before making his move. Then his hand snaked beneath the well-dressed man's coattail and plucked a bulging wallet from his hip pocket.

His timing was admirable, because in another few moments his victim would be on the bus, and the bus would be moving away. Even if the man reached for his wallet to pay his fare, it would be too late to do anything but fume. The bus wouldn't stop again for two blocks, and by the time the victim managed to run back to that corner, the little pickpocket would be long gone.

Except that not having eyes in the back of his head undid him. A quiet but deadly voice behind him said, "Put that in your pocket and you'll pull out a stump."

Coley froze, instantly recognizing the voice as that of Starsky. His reaction was a mixture of fear and astonishment. Starsky moved in on his left and Hutch moved in on his right. The little pickpocket's eyes flicked from one to the other in open-mouthed wonder.

"What are you two doin' here?" he asked in the tone of a man who had seen ghosts.

Hutch said in an admonishing voice, "We work here, Coley, but our work is legal. Now give the man back his wallet."

Licking his lips, the little man swung his attention back to the well-dressed man, who was next in line to a fat woman just getting on the bus. The pickpocket's hand snaked out again, and the wallet disappeared back into its owner's pocket as smoothly as it had come out. The well-dressed man got on the bus without ever realizing that for a few moments it had been gone.

Hutch said, "Let's take a walk."

He took the little man's right arm, Starsky took his left, and they strolled in the direction of Hutch's parked sedan.

Hutch said chidingly, "Coley, I thought we had an understanding. I'm disappointed in you."

Starsky said, "You said you'd never work our district while we were here. Remember?"

Nodding weakly, the little man said nothing. They halted next to the sedan, and Hutch pulled open the curbside front door.

"Then why did you go back on your word?" Hutch asked. "It's not nice to go back on your word. That's immoral, Coley."

The blond detective took Coley's right hand and wrapped the fingers about the upper rail of the open car door. He said regretfully, "I would hate to close the door on our relationship, Coley."

The little man attempted to jerk his hand away, but Hutch held it in a vise-like grip. "Hey, no," Coley said in a pleading tone. "I mean, I got hands like a surgeon's."

Hutch nodded. "At this point in time, yes, you do."

Coley threw Starsky a pleading look, got no help

there, and looked back at Hutch again. Mixed with his fear was a definite note of puzzlement.

"Look, isn't today the seventeenth?" he asked.

After considering, Starsky said, "Yeah. So what?"

Coley seemed to be contemplating a straight reply, then reconsidered and simply shook his head. "I was just asking, that's all. Now lemme go, okay? I won't work your district. Straight, I won't."

Starsky asked, "Why does the date matter, Coley?"

"It doesn't, it doesn't. Just let me walk. Come on. It'll take you the whole day to book me. You don't want to waste the whole day on a two-bit cannon like me, do you?"

He looked earnestly from one to the other. When the two detectives merely examined him expressionlessly, he suddenly had a thought that brightened him. "You got no evidence anyway. The mark's got his wallet back."

Starsky and Hutch exchanged glances. Hutch gripped the edge of the car door and made as though he intended to slam it. Coley let out a squeal of alarm. While his terrified gaze was fixed on the hand he expected to be mangled, Starsky slipped his own wallet into the man's side pocket.

"I wasn't trying to be smart," Coley said pleadingly. "Go ahead and book me if you want. Geeze, I'll confess even."

"What does the date matter, Coley?" Starsky repeated.

The little man merely gave his head a hopeless shake. Starsky and Hutch exchanged another glance, then both shrugged. Hutch released his hand and Starsky released his left arm. Emitting a sigh of relief, the pickpocket gave them an uncertain smile and started to walk away. Starsky grabbed him by the back of his coat collar and reeled him in like a trout.

Starsky patted his side coat pocket, dipped his hand

into it and brought out the wallet. He held it in front of Coley's nose. "Well, now, it looks as though we *do* have evidence after all, Coley. Enough to revoke your parole, throw you back in the joint, and add a couple of years."

The little man gazed at the wallet with a mixture of outrage and fear. "Aw, come on," he said. "You guys are too square to frame me."

"You got to fight fire with fire," Starsky told him. "We've hardened in the time you've been away. Why does the date matter?"

Coley sighed. "I got to report to my parole officer before five. That's all, honest."

Starsky and Hutch looked at each other. It was such a patent lie that both had pained expressions on their faces. But it was also obvious they were not going to get a straight answer from the little man. Hutch barely nodded, and Starsky released his grip. He slid the wallet back into his own pocket.

After glancing over his shoulder at them, Coley took a tentative step away. When there was no further move to stop him, he took another.

Before he could take a third, Starsky said quietly, "Coley."

Halting, the little man shuddered. He glanced over his shoulder fearfully.

Starsky said, "The next time you put your hand in someone else's pocket, the two of you better be engaged."

Coley gave a relieved nod. He took another tentative step, then another, and when there was no further challenge, hurried off at a brisk pace.

Watching the little man's retreat, Hutch said in a tone of dissatisfaction, "Coley must be taking hormone shots, or he never would have crossed us like that."

Equally dissatisfied, Starsky said, "And what's with the date bit?"

Shaking his head, Hutch said, "I don't know, but there's something going on that's making me a little antsy. Did you get the impression when he first looked at us that he was more surprised than scared?"

"More like astonished," Starsky said. "Like we were a pair of ghosts."

Hutch nodded. "There's something going on today that doesn't fit."

About that same time, Edith Dobey was reentering the master bedroom of her Los Angeles home after getting her fifteen-year-old son and eight-year-old daughter off to school. Her husband was lying on his back, arms outside the covers, patiently waiting for her. He was a large black man in his late forties, an inch short of six feet tall and weighing 225 pounds. He had a round, intelligent face and wore a black mustache. Most of the time his expression tended to be serious, but at the moment he was smiling widely.

The smile was because of his wife's performance. Kicking off her bedroom slippers, she began doing a stripper's strut alongside the bed. As she walked back and forth, bumping and grinding, she sensuously and gradually allowed the robe she wore over her nightgown to fall from her shoulders, and finally to the floor. She was an attractive woman several years younger than her husband, with a voluptuous figure, and watching her husband's increasingly turned-on expression from the corners of her eyes as she strutted back and forth was giving her considerable delight.

As she allowed one nightgown strap to slide down to expose a smooth black shoulder, her husband said, "I take it the kids are off—I hope."

She didn't even deign to reply to that inanity. The other shoulder strap slid off her shoulder, she performed a few more bumps and grinds, and the night-gown slithered to the floor. For a moment she held a pose, one hand behind her head, the other balled on a hip, back arched to make her bosom jut out. Then, as her husband began a rhythmic clapping, she giggled and jumped beneath the covers. She snuggled up against him and he put his arms around her. Sliding her arms about his neck, she raised her lips.

The phone rang.

Grunting in irritation, Dobey lifted the bedside extension and held it to his ear.

"Yeah?" he said.

"Captain Dobey?" a male voice inquired.

"Uh-huh."

"Mark Henderson of the District Attorney's office. I phoned your office, but they told me you wouldn't be in today."

"It's my day off," the captain said peevishly.

"Yes, I know. Ordinarily I wouldn't bother you, Captain, but a matter of some urgency has come up. Could you drop by my office as soon as possible?"

"Drop by your office? Just what is your capacity in the D.A.'s office, Mr. Henderson?"

"I'm an assistant district attorney."

"Oh." There was a moment of silence, then Dobey said, "Counselor, I just told you it's my day off."

"And I just told you I knew it," the assistant district attorney said in a steady tone. "Believe me, if it weren't urgent, I wouldn't have phoned you at home."

"Can't you tell me over the phone?" Dobey growled.

"No, I can't."

There was a continuing silence, finally broken by the captain emitting a resigned sigh. "All right, Counselor. Be there in a half-hour."

"Fine, Captain. Oh, incidentally, my office is in the Police Building, not at 210 West Temple. I'm the new liaison officer between the D.A.'s office and the L.A.P.D."

"What happened to Carlson?" Dobey asked.

"Went into private practice, Captain." He emitted a little chuckle. "Why we all don't, I don't know. That's where the money is."

"Yeah," the captain said dourly. "I've thought of becoming a private eye myself."

Hanging up, Captain Dobey savagely threw the covers back off both himself and his wife, swung his feet to the floor, and stood up. When he looked down at her naked body broodingly, she put both hands behind her head and arched her back.

"Don't make it even worse than it is," he growled at her.

Giving him an apologetic smile, she sat up, grabbed the covers, and pulled them up to her neck. She said, "Kids won't be home before two-thirty. There's lots of time."

"My luck, I'll probably get home at three," he said glumly, and headed for the shower.

Twenty-five minutes later, dressed in a conservatively dark suit, white shirt, and necktie, he pulled onto the Parker Center parking lot.

Inside he took one of the elevators to the sixth floor. He got off opposite the Traffic Bureau, turned right, and halted before a door lettered DISTRICT ATTORNEY'S LIAISON OFFICE. Below that, in smaller letters on a removable strip of plywood slid into a brass-edged frame, was lettered *Mark Henderson, Assistant District Attorney*.

Captain Dobey opened the door and went in.

Chapter 5

THE OFFICE WAS small and there was no secretary. Seated behind the desk was a handsome, well-built man in his early thirties with an Ivy League look about him. With his close-cropped hair, freshly scrubbed appearance, and immaculately pressed gray suit, he reminded Captain Dobey of some pre-Watergate presidential aide.

When the man looked up inquiringly, the black man said, "You Mark Henderson?"

"Yes."

"I'm Dobey."

Smiling, the assistant district attorney rose from his chair and extended his hand across the desk. "I appreciate your coming down here on your day off, Captain Dobey."

Gripping the hand briefly, then dropping it again, the captain growled, "You know, Counselor, I was enjoying doing what I was doing when I got your call. And the lady I was with was enjoying it, too. So leaving made me unhappy, and I am likely to stay unhappy unless your reason for getting me down here was a damn fine one."

Mark Henderson looked somewhat startled, obviously unused to such bluntness. He retained his smile, but it became a trifle forced. "I don't know that I can

31

make you happy, Captain, but I doubt that you'll be bored. It concerns two of your men. Detective Starsky and Detective Hutchinson."

"What about Starsky and Hutch?"

"We have reason to believe that someone is trying to kill them."

After gazing at him for a moment, Captain Dobey pulled back a chair sitting in front of the desk, sank into it, and folded his hands in his lap. "Well, now, Counselor, I have to concede that's one damn fine reason for interrupting my day off. Tell me about it."

The assistant district attorney resumed his seat, placed his elbows on the desk, and leaned forward. "First, a young couple parked on a beach north of Santa Monica was murdered by what we believe were two sawed-off shotguns, about twelve forty-five this morning. We know the time, because the shots could be heard a quarter mile away. We figure it was magnum ammo. Definitely a pro job."

"What's that got to do with Starsky and Hutch?" Dobey inquired.

"The car was a new Torino, red with a white stripe, identical to the car driven by Detective Starsky." After a pause he added, "That coincidence was brought to my attention by Detective Ballin of Homicide, a member of the team investigating the double murder."

Captain Dobey stared at him. "You must have more than that, Counselor."

"Of course. Just before I phoned you, I got a call from Detective Ballin. He had just received a phone call from what he referred to as a snitch. I gathered that's police jargon for an informer."

The captain regarded him curiously. "How long you been with the D.A.'s office, Counselor?"

"Four years." When Captain Dobey seemed bemused by this information, he added explanatorily, "Prior to this assignment, I was in the fraud and embezzlement section. My experience has been largely with white-collar criminals."

"I see," Dobey said, nodding. "What did Ballin's snitch say?"

"It's all over the street that a contract has been put out on Detective Hutchinson and Detective Starsky. It was only after receiving that call that the coincidence of the cars occurred to Detective Ballin. He suggested that the murderers thought they were killing Starsky."

Captain Dobey heaved himself to his feet. "I'll have Starsky and Hutch pulled in off the street. Soon as they get here, I'll let you know, and you can come down to my office to explain all this to them."

"Fine, Captain," Henderson said with a nod. "I'll be waiting for your call."

The brown Ford was still cruising. Since their unsatisfactory conference with the pickpocket, Starsky and Hutch had stopped and shaken down a known heroin dealer (unsuccessfully), had broken up a street corner fight, and had twice stopped for idle chitchat with street people—once with a prostitute, once with a numbers runner—just to inquire if anything unusual was going on in the district.

Both sensed that something was, but they were unable to put their fingers on just what. They had gotten no particular reaction from the street fighters, who were strangers to them; but the dealer, the hooker, and the runner, who were not, all had looked startled to see them, uneasy to be in their presence, and relieved when they moved on. That was understandable with the dealer, since they had shaken him down, but they had made it clear to the other two that all they wanted was conversation.

For a time after their contact with the numbers runner they cruised without incident. Moving along slowly, they missed nothing going on either side of

the street, but spotted nothing out of place and no
street people they considered it worthwhile to stop
and talk to.

After a long period of silent cruising, Starsky finally
said, "You know, still bugs me how surprised to see
us Coley was."

Hutch said, "Well, Coley's only been out for a
couple of months. Maybe somebody gave him a bum
steer that we were transferred or something."

"Yeah, but what about all the other looks we've
been getting? Everybody can't think we're transferred."

Hutch had stopped listening because his attention
was centered on a short fat man loitering in front of
a plate-glass window with gold lettering on it—COOS
BAY TAVERN—6:00 A.M. TO 2:00 A.M. The man was
hard to miss. About fifty, he wore a small goatee, a
red bandanna across his forehead, and a T-shirt with
a picture of a heart with a dagger through it and the
inscription *Born to Raise Hell.*

The fat man spotted Hutch looking at him at the
same moment the blond man saw him. His mouth fell
open, his eyes grew wide, and he instantly turned into
the tavern.

At the moment there was no traffic other than the
undercover cruiser going back and forth along the
street. After a glance in his side-view mirror, Hutch
spun the wheel to send the car into a tight U-turn. The
sudden movement hurled Starsky against the door.

Throwing his partner a startled look, Starsky said,
"What's going on, man?"

"Fat Rolly over there," Hutch said. "Spotted us,
then ran into the place like a bottomless dancer with
the trots."

Starsky's interest perked up. "Might be the same
thing that got Coley and everybody else so itchy."

The car screeched to a halt in a no-parking zone in

front of the tavern, and the detectives spilled out either side. But as they headed for the tavern entrance, an announcement from their car radio stopped them short.

"Cruiser Three, come in, please," the radio voice said. "Cruiser Three, come in."

Starsky and Hutch looked at each other. Starsky inclined his head toward the tavern door, indicating that they should forget the radio. But Hutch, who tended to operate a bit more by the book than his partner, couldn't resist the radio call any more than most people can resist a ringing phone.

Running back to lean into the front seat and bring out the microphone, Hutch said, "Three here. What is it?"

The dispatcher said, "Cruiser Three, the following from Dobey. He wants you back in here. Urgent, and immediate."

Hutch looked at Starsky and made a face. He started to open the car door to climb back under the wheel, but Starsky grabbed the mike from his hand.

Hitting the transmit button, Starsky said, "Dispatch, you better say that again. Our radio's been acting up. Sometimes we can't hardly make out a thing."

He tossed the microphone into the front seat. Grinning, Hutch clicked his door closed again and followed Starsky into the tavern.

Behind them the radio said, "Roger, Cruiser Three. The following message from Dobey. Report to his office immediately."

The bar was small, but well patronized even though it was not quite ten in the morning. It was so dimly lighted that it took a few moments for the detectives' vision to adjust. When they were finally able to make out their surroundings, they saw that about a dozen customers were lined up at the bar. Fat Rolly was not one of them.

Then Starsky pointed toward the rear of the room. A fat, short figure stood in the phone booth, just closing the phone book. The two detectives moved swiftly in that direction.

Most of the bar patrons had looked around when they entered. As they passed behind the bar stools, the detectives were conscious of looks following them, but they were too intent on the man in the phone booth to note any expressions.

Fat Rolly had deposited a coin and was just completing his dialing when Starsky slid the booth door open. The fat man threw a startled glance over his shoulder, then instantly hung up. The phone hadn't rung long enough for anyone on the other end to answer, because there was the sound of the dime clinking into the return box.

Reaching past the fat man, Starsky retrieved the dime.

Hutch said congenially, "Hi, Rolly. How's it going?"

"Great, Hutch," Rolly said with eager camaraderie, his expression denoting unexpected pleasure at seeing both detectives, but his quivering chins giving away the fraud. "Supersensational. How's it going with you guys?"

Starsky said, "Fine, just fine, Rolly. Here's your dime."

He held the coin in front of Rolly's nose. Giving him a weak smile of thanks, the fat man took it and dropped it into a pocket.

Starsky said, "So anxious to talk to us, you couldn't even wait to complete your call, huh?"

Rolly's smile became even weaker. "Well, I—I forgot the number."

"In the middle of dialing?" Hutch asked with raised eyebrows. "That's a little unusual, isn't it, Rolly?"

"I—." Rolly mentally probed for some plausible excuse, gave up, and merely shrugged.

All this time he had been standing in the phone booth. Now he moved out, a trifle cautiously, glanced from Hutch to Starsky, then averted his gaze from both.

Hutch said, "Seemed to me you were surprised to see us when we cruised by outside, Rolly."

"Me?" the fat man said with wide-eyed innocence. "Why would I be surprised?"

"What we wondered," Hutch said.

Starsky was frowning in the direction of the bar. "Hold it, Hutch," he said.

Looking that way, too, Hutch saw that everyone at the bar, including the bartender, was watching them. But it wasn't just idle curiosity. They were being examined with the same air of surprise and apprehension they were beginning to become accustomed to.

Hutch was merely bemused, but Starsky began to get angry. He said, "I can take looks like that from one or two, but this is getting out of hand."

"So what do we do about it?" Hutch asked.

"I don't know what you're going to do, but I'm going to find out what the hell this is all about. And right now."

He moved determinedly in the direction of the bar.

Chapter 6

STARSKY MOVED RIGHT behind the bar, ignoring the scowl of the bartender, an oversized man with a low forehead and hairy arms. Leaning his elbows on the back bar next to the cash register, the detective ran his gaze over the bar patrons. They gazed back at him with a mixture of hostility and uneasiness, rather as tigers regard an animal trainer who walks through their cage.

Starsky opened his mouth to speak, paused when he felt his left elbow pressing against something on the back bar, and glanced down at it. It was a drinking glass full of pencils.

That gave him an idea that changed the course of his thinking. Picking up the glass and setting it on the front bar, he glanced around until he spotted a pile of cocktail napkins, and set them next to the glass. Then he clapped his hands for attention, an unnecessary gesture since he already had the silent attention of everyone in the place.

In the loud, bright voice of a host attempting to liven up a dull party, he said, "All right, folks! All right! Looks to me like we've got to open up some lines of communication here. Now you all know me and Hutch." He pointed toward the rear of the place. "That's Hutch back there with glut-gut Rolly. And you know we're cops. And we know you know, and we know you don't like us, but T.S., friends, that's the way it is."

The entire delivery was upbeat and happy, yet somehow deadly. He began moving along the bar, elbowing the hairy-armed bartender aside, placing a napkin in front of each patron and a pencil next to each napkin. He gave each person a smile, but it was only his lips that smiled. Looking into his eyes was like gazing into the barrels of twin dueling pistols.

None of the customers met his gaze squarely. Several shot tentative glances toward the door, but seemed to decide that attempting to leave right then might be riskier than staying.

As he delivered the napkins, he continued to talk. "All morning people have been looking at us like Lazarus the day after, and it's starting to get to us. You follow? So that's the question—what's so special about two cops patroling the district they've been patroling every day for the past three years? Now somebody in here knows, and that's what we want to find out, you see."

Placing a napkin and pencil before the last customer, he walked back to where the bartender stood sullenly leaning against the back bar and held out a napkin and a pencil to him. "So if each of you will just write down what you think might be the reason—." He let it hang, waiting for the bartender to accept the napkin and pencil.

Making no move to take either, the bartender asked with faint belligerence, "Suppose I don't feel like writing anything down?"

Starsky smiled from the teeth out. "Well, then, friend, you'll end up looking like you've been bobbing for apples in a tub full of strawberry jam."

The bartender looked into Starsky's eyes, his gaze shifted to the proffered napkin and pencil, and he decided to accept both. Placing the napkin on the back bar, he cupped it with his left hand to shield what he was writing, and began to scribble something. Starsky headed back toward the end of the bar nearest the rear, where Hutch and Fat Rolly were now standing.

Handing the fat man a napkin, he said, "Sorry, Rolly. Out of pencils."

"Guess I can't do it, then," the fat man said. "Got none, either."

Hutch dipped a hand into his sport jacket and came out with a ballpoint pen. He handed it to Rolly. Accepting it with reluctance, Rolly cupped his hand about the napkin and began to write.

In the same bright, party-giving tone as before, Starsky announced generally, "Twenty-five words or less will do. Neatness and originality will be taken into consideration."

An aging, heavily painted hooker at the bar asked sarcastically, "What's first prize?"

"A hundred thousand units of penicillin, sweetheart. Share it with your friends."

Glaring at him, the women's lips formed the words, "Screw you," but the message was soundless.

Fat Rolly finished his writing and folded the napkin in half. He handed it to Starsky and returned Hutch's pen to him. Glancing along the bar, Starsky saw that everyone had finished writing and had similarly folded their napkins in half. He began moving along the bar collecting them, chattering cheerfully as he went.

"Thank you. And thank you for your kindness. Thank you, sir. Bless you, madam. Thank you very much. Your reward will come in the next life, I'm sure. Thank you."

He collected the bartender's entry last. Moving back to the end of the bar from which he had started, he divided the pile of folded napkins into two equal stacks and handed half to Hutch. Both began opening them and reading.

"People look at you funny because cops smell," Starksy read aloud, then glanced along the bar. "There's no prize for the stupidest answer."

Hutch also read aloud. "We heard you got suspended for catching clap." Looking at the aging hooker, he said, "That sounds like repartee for my partner's crack, beautiful."

"If it fits, wear it," she told him.

Sighing, Starsky unfolded another napkin. To himself, but loudly enough for everyone to hear, he said, "We just may have to close this place down unless we find what we're looking for."

"Close it down?" the bartender said on a high note. "On what grounds?"

Starsky looked at him. "Public safety code 2377. Every open sewer is supposed to have a manhole cover."

"Here it is!" Hutch said. "Pay dirt!"

He handed an unfolded napkin to Starsky. After quickly scanning the message written on it, Starsky gave his partner a wide-eyed look. "Says I was supposed to have been killed last night."

Hutch looked at Fat Rolly. "And it says it in red ink, exactly like the ballpoint pen I just loaned Fat Rolly."

Starsky looked at the fat man, too, who seemed to be trying to shrink inward in order to make himself less noticeable. Starsky gave him a bleak grin. Rounding the end of the bar to the customer side, he took a grip on the flab of Rolly's upper arm.

"You win first prize, gashole," he said. "Come on."

He steered the fat man toward the rearmost booth. Hutch, still standing at the bar, crooked his finger at the bartender.

When the man came over, Hutch slapped a quarter

down on the bar. "Give me three double Scotches, and here's a quarter for the juke box."

"We don't have no juke box," the man said sullenly.

"Then stick the quarter in your ear, sing 'Danny Boy,' and get three double Scotches."

At the booth Starsky pushed Fat Rolly in next to the wall, slid in next to him, and was crowding close in a deliberate attempt to give the fat man a hemmed-in feeling.

"Okay, Rolly," he said. "Who was supposed to kill me?"

"I don't know, Starsky," the fat man said earnestly. "On my mother's life, I don't know."

"You don't have a mother. They found you in the garbage can behind Weight Watchers. Again, *who*?"

Rolly took the red bandanna from around his forehead and wiped his suddenly perspiring face with it. "I don't know. Just street talk. Everybody heard there was a contract out on you, that it was supposed to be last night. I don't know who, or where, or when. It was just, you know, a kind of rumor."

Hutch came over carrying three double Scotches on the rocks. Setting them down, he seated himself across from the other two, shoved one glass before Rolly, one before Starsky, and kept the third. Rolly immediately picked up his and gulped down half of it in one swallow. The two detectives let theirs lie.

Starsky said to Hutch, "Rolly says there was a contract out. Just street talk so far. Nothing to back it up."

Hutch said sadly, "Starsky, I think Rolly isn't being completely honest with us."

"I am so," Rolly said.

Hutch turned suddenly glittering eyes on him. "Because when you saw us outside, you headed right for the phone, Rolly. I sure would like to know who you were calling."

Rolly used the bandanna to wipe his face again. "I

was calling—" He searched wildly for someone plausible, then finished on a note of triumph, "—my bookie, that's who."

"What were you betting on, Rolly?" Starsky shot at him.

"Basketball game," the fat man said promptly. "Lakers and Knicks."

Right on top of the fat man, Hutch said, "What kind of point spread the bookie give you?"

"Knicks plus four," Rolly said quickly.

Starsky and Hutch both turned wolfish grins on him. Starsky asked softly, "How'd he give it to you when you didn't complete the call?"

That stopped the fat man cold. His mouth opened and closed like a fish kissing the side of a bowl. He picked up his drink and downed the rest of it. As he set down the glass, Hutch slid his across the table to him. Nodding his gratitude, Rolly downed half of that one, too.

Hutch said, "See, Rolly, you're not furthering police-community relations when you don't tell us everything you know. That makes us surly, Rolly."

Rolly drank the rest of Hutch's drink. Starsky slid his glass over in front of him. The fat man tossed off half of it.

In the tone of a teacher reasoning with a recalcitrant child, Starsky said, "One thing you ought to remember about me and Hutch. We're not like most partners. Usually there's one guy who's the hard-nose, rough-'em-up kind of guy. And then the other partner is kind of like Pat O'Brien, folksy, always wants the best for everybody. Well, that doesn't work for Hutch and me." His tone suddenly became menacing. "We're both hard-nosed, Rolly, and we don't like people who don't tell us everything they know."

Rolly finished off the third drink, set down the glass next to the other two, and patted his cheeks with the red bandanna. He seemed slightly surprised that he had stopped sweating. Bunching the bandanna and shoving it into a pocket, he gazed blearily from one detective to the other.

The Scotch seemed to have given him courage, because he said with alcoholic bravado, "I told you all I'm going to tell you."

Hutch emitted a regretful sigh. "Then I'm afraid we're going to have to put you under arrest."

"Under arrest?" Rolly said in a high voice. "What for?"

Hutch pointed to the three empty glasses. "Public drunkenness, Rolly. You've had six Scotches in five minutes."

The fat man looked down at the empty glasses lined up in front of him, then up at Hutch and at Starsky. Both detectives smiled cheerfully. Sliding from the booth, Starsky took the fat man's arm and jerked him out of it. Hutch rose from the booth, too.

"You pay?" Starsky asked his partner.

Hutch shook his head.

"I'll catch it," Starsky said. "You take charge of lard-bucket."

Nodding, Hutch steered the fat man, weaving slightly, in the direction of the door. Pulling a crumpled wad of bills from his pocket, Starsky moved over to the bar. It was now deserted—everyone had quietly left while the two detectives were busy with Fat Rolly.

"Okay," Starsky said to the bartender. "What do we owe you?"

The man shook his head. "Nothin', Officer. Not for you two."

Starsky's right hand shot across the bar to grip the man's shirt front and jerk him belly-down halfway across the bar. In a low, hard voice, he said directly into the bartender's face, "Three double Scotches should total four dollars and fifty cents. Add a fifty-cent tip, and that's an even five. And if you ever try to put me and Hutch on the cuff again, I'm going to buy you a barbed-wire cummerbund and give you a custom fitting."

Releasing his grip, he tossed a five-dollar bill on the bar and started for the door. Just before reaching it, he paused and turned. In a warm voice belied by his cold smile, he said, "Always nice talking to you."

He went on out.

Chapter 7

STARSKY SAT in the back seat with Fat Rolly, while Hutch drove the Ford. The prisoner wasn't handcuffed —it was customary to handcuff drunks only if they became violent.

Before pulling away from the no-parking zone, Hutch lifted the radio microphone and said into it, "Cruiser Three to Control One. Come in, Control One."

A voice from the speaker said, "Control One to Cruiser Three. I've been trying to transmit to you for the last half-hour."

"Radio's been acting up," Hutch said. "Seems to be working now."

"Urgent message from Captain Dobey, Cruiser Three. You are to report to his office immediately."

"Roger, Control One," Hutch said. "Cruiser Three over and out."

He hung up the microphone.

From ingrained habit, both detectives continued to scan their surroundings all the way to Parker Center. Even as they pulled onto the parking lot, their gazes continued to take in everything around them. As they started past the fence with a large sign on it reading IMPOUND VEHICLES, Starsky stiffened at sight of a red and white Torino the other side of the fence.

Leaning forward to tap his partner's shoulder, he said, "Hutch, hold it a second."

Braking to a halt, Hutch threw an inquiring glance over his shoulder.

"They've got my heap in Impound," Starsky said, climbing from the car. "Looks like it's minus a windshield, too."

He walked over to the gate and pushed through. Hutch stayed in the car, but the fence wasn't a dozen feet away, and the Torino was pulled up right next to it. Hutch leaned over to wind down the passenger-side window so that he could talk to his partner.

Starsky halted in front of the car. "Not my license," he announced. He bent to peer into the interior through the open space where the windshield had been. In a surprised voice he said, "Not my car."

"You sure?" Hutch said. "Didn't think there was another wild as yours in the whole town."

"One, apparently." Starsky bent to look into the car again. "Rear window missing, too. And blood all over the front seat. Shotguns, looks like. Point blank."

Hutch said, "Must have been magnum shells to take out the rear window."

"Uh-huh. And my guess is 00 buckshot." He studied the damaged vehicle contemplatively. "Car's too low to see into without bending down. They probably never even saw who they were killing. That's a stinking crime."

Hutch said, "Trying to kill you, you mean?"

Starsky looked at him through the wire fence. "If I mistook it for my own, no reason killers wouldn't. Probably dark, too."

He walked back through the gate and returned to the car. As he climbed into the back seat again, he said to Rolly, "Know anything about that, Rolly?"

The fat man shook his head.

Hutch, his body shifted sideways to look into the

back seat, said, "Come on, Rolly. You heard that Starsky got killed last night. You called it a rumor, but it had to be more definite than that, or you wouldn't have damn near given birth when you spotted us. You didn't hear that the hit was while he was driving his red and white Torino?"

The fat man held up his right hand, palm out. "God's truth, I didn't hear nothing except there'd been a hit. I already told you I didn't hear where, when, or why."

Facing forward again, Hutch drove on to the underground police garage and down the ramp. Halting alongside the vehicle dispatcher, he climbed out, leaving the engine running, and said to the dispatcher, "Suspect for booking. Park it somewhere, and we'll be back for it in a while."

Starsky and Fat Rolly got out of the back seat. The two detectives, one on either side of the prisoner, steered him to the elevator. They took it to the fourth floor, where Fat Rolly was given both a breath test and a blood test. Both showed an alcohol level legally constituting intoxication.

Taking the elevator back down to the first floor, they led Rolly to the booking desk in the jail.

"You guys really going to go through with this?" the fat man asked querulously as Starsky began to fill out the necessary forms.

Hutch said, "Feel like telling us the *whole* story, Rolly? Like who bought the hit?"

"Geeze, how many times I got to tell you guys I don't know?"

Starsky finished filling out the forms, signed them, and gave them to the booking sergeant. "He'll probably make bond," he said. "Give us a call at Captain Dobey's office if he does, huh?"

"Sure," the sergeant said.

Starsky and Hutch took the elevator again, this time

49

to the third floor, and entered Captain Dobey's office. The captain barked a greeting. "You sure took your time!"

"We were pursuing a suspect when the message came over the radio, Captain," Hutch said.

"A suspect for what?" the captain asked skeptically.

"You name it," Hutch said. "He's a fence, a procurer, a finger man, and he's rumored to be a contact man for most anything you want, up to and including people willing to commit murder for a fee."

Captain Dobey looked somewhat mollified. "What were you pursing him for?"

Hutch looked at Starsky, who accepted the passed buck by saying, "Just a misdemeanor this time, Captain."

"What misdemeanor?" the captain asked patiently.

Starsky glanced at Hutch, throwing the buck back to him. Clearing his throat, Hutch said, "Public drunkenness."

"What!" Dobey roared. "You kept me sitting here on my day off while you chased down a common drunk!"

Starsky said to Hutch, "Why didn't you just stick to the bad reception excuse? Control One bought it."

The captain began to puff up as though on the verge of bursting. Hutch said hurriedly and soothingly, "It's not like it sounds, Captain. We were trying to squeeze information out of him on a felony."

After glaring from one to the other, the captain emitted a resigned snort and pointed to a couple of chairs in front of his desk. "Sit."

Obediently the two detectives sat and folded their hands in their laps. Captain Dobey picked up the phone on his desk and dialed only three numbers, which meant he was calling an extension within the building.

After a moment he said into the phone, "Captain

Dobey here, Counselor. Starsky and Hutchinson finally rolled in. Can you come down now? . . . Fine." He hung up.

"Counselor?" Starsky ventured.

"Mark Henderson, the new liaison man from the D.A.'s office," the captain said in a tone containing none of the anger of a moment before. "Wants to talk to you two."

"Well, well," Starsky said. "The glamour boy of the D.A.'s office. Harvard Law School, father is a partner in one of Manhattan's most prestigious law firms, family used to be one of the four hundred, back when there was still something called High Society."

"How do you know so much about him?" Hutch asked curiously.

"Sunday paper. Big write-up."

Captain Dobey said, "I didn't see it."

"Society section," Starsky explained. "He's getting married."

Hutch examined his partner with a look of wonder. "You read the society section?"

"Sure."

"Why?"

"Because I read the whole damn paper."

After considering this, Hutch said, "Everything?"

"Even Heloise," Starsky assured him.

Captain Dobey asked, "Who's the prospective bride?"

"Chick named Deborah something-or-other. I forget, except her father's a bank president and they live in Beverly Hills."

"I guess he's not marrying out of his class, then," Hutch said dryly.

The door opened and Mark Henderson came in. Captain Dobey made introductions all around, and the two detectives rose to their feet to offer handshakes.

After gripping their hands, the assistant district attorney said, "Keep your seats, gentlemen. This won't take long."

Pointing to a chair against the wall, Captain Dobey said, "Take that chair over there, Counselor."

"Thanks, but I think better on my feet," Henderson said.

Starsky and Hutch turned their chairs around to face the man, so that their backs wouldn't be to him. Henderson clasped his hands behind his back, looking very much like a professor beginning a class lecture.

In a tone meant to impress, he said, "We have reason to believe that someone tried to kill Detective Starsky last night."

"Yeah, we know," Starsky said offhandedly.

Henderson stared at him. "You know?"

"It's all over the street." Starsky turned to the captain. "That's what we were chasing the drunk about. We thought he'd know something about it. In fact we *know* he knows more than he's telling us."

"Who's that?" Henderson asked.

"A five-by-five fence named Fat Rolly. Currently in the can on a drunk charge. But it wouldn't do you any good to talk to him, Counselor. If Hutch and I can't pry him open, nobody can."

Henderson was silent for a few moments. Then he said wryly, "You've stolen my thunder. But maybe not all of it. Do you know about the young couple murdered in a car identical to Starsky's last night?"

Starsky said, "We saw a shotgun-blasted Torino in the Impound lot and figured it was something like that. We don't know any details, though. How young a couple?"

"The boy was twenty-two and the girl nineteen."

Starsky and Hutch both made faces.

"The car was stolen, presumably by the boy, since he was in the driver's seat. It's registered to a Terrance

Crowder in the Boyle Heights district. Hadn't been reported stolen, because he didn't even know it was gone from the carport until the cops woke him up about two this morning."

Hutch asked, "Sure he wasn't covering himself, and actually had loaned it?"

"Why would he do that?" Henderson asked. "He couldn't have had any connection with the killers. For that matter, neither could the kid who stole the car, or his girl friend. Homicide figures it was simply a mistake in identity on the killers' part. It's Homicide's theory that they spotted the Torino, thought it was Starsky out with a girl, followed the car, and killed the two young people, thinking they were getting Starsky." He gave Starsky a small smile. "It's my understanding it wouldn't be unusual for your partner to be seen with a girl."

Starsky jerked a thumb toward his blond partner on the opposite side of the desk. "I'm Starsky. That's Hutch."

"Oh, sorry," Henderson said in an embarrassed voice.

Starsky asked, "Where was the hit?"

"A deserted public beach north of Santa Monica. They were parked and—ah—"

Starsky nodded. "I probably know the beach. I've been known to park there, and maybe the killers knew it, too."

Hutch asked, "Homicide have any theories about who the killers were?"

"Not the actual killers. They figure they were hired pros."

"Hired by whom?"

Henderson said, "Gerald Tallman, is my theory. To stop you from testifying against him." He looked at Dobey. "I know it sounds like a long shot, Captain, just because the car involved was the same as Starsky here drives." He nodded toward Hutch. "But—"

"I'm Hutch," the blond man interrupted, jerking his thumb toward his partner. "That's Starsky."

Chapter 8

To save Henderson the embarrassment of apologizing for a second time, Captain Dobey quickly put in to Starsky, "What the Counselor is pointing out is that you're not the only one who drives that kind of car."

"Close, I'd say, Captain. That's a custom paint job, so this Crowder guy's must be, too. Has to be sheerest coincidence that he got one just like mine."

"Maybe not," Hutch said. "Maybe he saw yours on the street and liked it. Some people have lousy taste."

"No danger of anybody copying that brown job of yours," Starsky said, grinning at him. "Nobody has taste that lousy." He turned back to Henderson. "I'd say it might be a case of mistaken identity, but it wouldn't be Tallman."

Henderson frowned. "Together your testimony can convict him of eight counts of bribery. Don't you think that's sufficient motive?"

Hutch said, "Yeah, he's got sufficient motive, but he's also sufficiently bright not to take us on that way."

"Who else, then?" Captain Dobey asked.

Both men looked thoughtful. In a tone more like someone trying to recall old schoolmates than trying to dredge from his memory the names of people who might be interested in killing him and Starsky, Hutch said, "The Kulman brothers. They'd mulch us if they got the chance."

Starsky nodded. "What about the guy with the bad breath? Walks with a limp."

"Pucker? Yeah, he'd take a shot."

Starsky said, "Kelly and Parks worked together. They might team up again to take a crack at splashing us."

Henderson looked from one to the other, then turned his incredulous gaze at Dobey in silent inquiry as to whether this ongoing list of possible assassins was on the up and up, or if the pair were putting him on. Dobey gave him a bare nod to indicate that it was the former.

"Paindexter p.o.'d enough?" Hutch asked.

Starsky shook his head. "Not if he's off the sauce."

"He'll never quit. He's a juicer till he dies."

Henderson broke in. "Well, one thing's definite. You're off the street until after the Tallman trial. For your own good."

Looking up at him, Starsky said evenly, "Mr. Henderson, you better suck that up and blow it out again, because that bird ain't *never* going to fly."

The vernacular, the tone, and the expression on Starsky's face all astonished the assistant district attorney. In an offended voice he said, "I beg your pardon?"

Hutch said, "We've got a schedule to keep, Counselor. Maybe you don't know that, but there are a lot of places we have to be. We have a very important stakeout to run tonight. We have to meet Huggy Bear to see if he's turned anything for us."

Captain Dobey said, "Who the hell is Huggy Bear?"

"Guy runs a bar," Starsky said. "Generally knows everything happening on the street."

"A snitch?"

Starsky shook his head. "Friend of ours. Whatever

street information Huggy Bear gives is strictly for friendship. He's not for sale."

The captain's phone rang. He picked it up and said, "Dobey. . . . Okay, I'll tell them."

Hanging up, he said to Starsky and Hutch, "That drunk you brought in, he got in touch with a bondsman, and they're processing him out right now. They said you wanted to know."

Hutch was on his feet and moving for the door before the captain finished speaking. He tossed his keys to Starsky.

"I'll cover him," he said. "You go back to Vinnie's and get the Torino. Nice to have met you, Mr. Henderson."

"Now wait just a minute!" Henderson said.

But he was speaking to a closed door. Henderson gave Dobey a look of appeal, but got only a shrug in reply.

Coming to his feet, Starsky asked politely of both men, "Will that be all?"

Henderson glanced at Dobey again, got no help there, and surrendered gracefully. "May I ask why you're changing cars?"

"To let whoever it is know that it didn't work."

Henderson considered this and obviously didn't like it. "To decoy them into another try?"

"Something like that."

Henderson sighed. "Can we reach some kind of compromise? Will you at least agree to keep us notified of your whereabouts throughout the day?"

"Every half-hour," Starsky said agreeably.

"Every fifteen minutes," Henderson said firmly.

"Okay," Starsky said, shrugging. "Fifteen minutes, then."

He glanced at the captain, caught a faint smile on his face, and gave him an equally faint smile in return.

They both knew Starsky had no intention of phoning in at all, let alone on a definite schedule.

Starsky moved to the door, but paused and turned with his hand on the knob. In a tone that was neither sarcastic nor insulting, but merely explanatory, he said, "See, what you guys don't understand is that Hutch and me are willing to risk getting burned out on the street, but it would hurt like hell if we lost while sitting on our butts in this office."

He walked out and closed the door behind him.

Mark Henderson sank into the chair Dobey had originally offered him. In a wondering voice he said, "Those two are suicidal."

The captain said, "A shrink might say that. Internal Affairs would say their methods are unorthodox. Public Relations would say they're surly and truculent and do not help the police image." He smiled briefly, and somehow chillingly. "All I know is that they're going looking for the guys who tried to kill Starsky, and if I was either of those guys, I'd make damn sure the blood bank laid in a good supply of my type."

Henderson ran uncertain fingers over his closely cropped hair. "They still strike me as suicidal, Captain."

Captain Dobey said quietly, "Maybe, but those two are also my best, Counselor." He stood up. "Any further developments and you can reach me at home." He glanced at his watch. "Guess I'm going to make it with plenty of leeway before two-thirty after all."

"What's at two-thirty?" Henderson asked, puzzled.

"My two children come home from school."

"Oh, and you like to be there to greet them?"

"Not exactly," Dobey said. "I like to be there at least an hour before greeting time."

Downstairs at the jail Hutch was asking the booking sergeant if Fat Rolly had been released yet. The sergeant shook his head.

"Bond's been posted, and all he has to do is sign for his personal effects. Right now he's taking his shower. We like to send them home clean, you know."

"He'll be a while, then," Hutch said. "He's got about an acre of skin to wash."

He walked over to where a row of phones rested on a narrow shelf against one wall. In block letters above the phones a number of notices were painted on the wall: NO SMOKING—LOITERING FORBIDDEN—OUTSIDE LINE DIAL 8—DO NOT DEFACE THESE WALLS. Under the last notice were a dozen penned and penciled comments about jail life, ranging from *Garbage fed here* to *Screw the screws*.

A half-dozen of the phones were being used by bondsmen, lawyers, and newly released prisoners. The one on the far left was vacant, and Hutch took it.

He dialed 8, then the seven digits of a number. The phone rang several times before a male voice finally said, "Chez Huggy Bear's. Angie the chef speaking."

"This is Hutch, Angie," Hutch said. "Put Huggy Bear on."

"Ain't here, Hutch."

"When you expect him back?"

"Not till morning. Gone to Catalina."

"Nuts," Hutch said. "What time in the morning?"

"Early," Angie answered. "But I wouldn't count on him being up and about. Little bomb he took with him, looked like he ain't gonna get much sleep. Probably hit the sack soon as he gets home. Try him about noon."

"Noon, hell," Hutch said. "This is important. You tell Huggy that Starsky and I will be there at eight-thirty sharp, and we want him alive."

"He ain't gonna like that," Angie said doubtfully. "Gonna need his beauty sleep."

"Huggy's already beautiful," Hutch said. "Just give him the message."

Hanging up, Hutch glanced over at the booking desk. The desk sergeant was in the process of emptying the contents of a manila envelope in front of Fat Rolly. Rolly was again wearing the red bandanna tied around his forehead, but it was now wrinkled and sweat-stained from being used as a face mop. Hutch watched as Rolly checked over his personal items and signed a receipt.

After stuffing the items into his pockets, Rolly waddled over to the bank of phones. He took the one on the far right, not noticing Hutch among the other phone users. Hutch watched him dial a number, then circled around behind him.

The fat man was saying into the phone, "Not my fault. Pushed the drinks on me, then busted me for drinking them."

Becoming conscious of someone standing behind him, the fat man glanced over his shoulder at Hutch and instantly hung up. He turned around to face the detective with a forced smile.

"Hello, Rolly," Hutch said easily. "Calling your bookie again?"

Shaking his head, Rolly said, "Calling my mother. Want her to know I might be a little bit late for din-din."

He started to move past Hutch, but the blond detective moved to block his way.

"What now?" Rolly asked warily.

"Has the name of the guy who bought the hit on Starsky occurred to you yet?"

"I told you everything I know, Hutch. Get off my back, huh?"

"Tell you what, Rolly," Hutch said. "We'll give you

twenty-four hours to think it over. If you phone in the name of the guy who wants me and Starsky dead by then, we won't knock over your secondhand store."

"That's a legitimate business," Rolly protested.

"It's so full of hot goods, we could get you on at least a hundred counts of receiving stolen property," Hutch told him. "You'll come out about in time to vote in the 1980 presidential election."

Rolly licked his lips. "Geeze, you don't have to pressure me for info, Hutch. I'd give it out of friendship, if I had it. You know that. Tell you what. I'll ask around, and if I turn anything, I'll phone you. Okay?" He looked at the detective hopefully.

Hutch gave his head a slow shake. "If you don't turn anything, kiss your little fence business good-bye, Rolly. And start packing for a vacation in the joint."

He turned and walked away.

While waiting at the entrance to the parking lot for Starsky to pick him up, Hutch mentally reviewed his conversation with Fat Rolly. Something that had happened kept tickling a corner of his mind, but when he attempted to focus on it, it eluded him.

The red and white Torino zoomed halfway into the "In" driveway and screeched to a halt next to Hutch. As Hutch climbed into the front seat next to Starsky, his partner dropped the keys to the brown Ford into his lap.

Pocketing them, Hutch said, "Check list?"

Backing out into the street, Starsky said, "I ran the check before I pulled off of Vinnie's parking lot."

Hutch nevertheless began a recheck as the car started forward. He glanced into the glove compartment, pulled the rack out from under the front seat and studied its contents, took the chained book from the dashboard, then slammed it back in place again.

Glancing sideways at him, Starsky asked, "What's eating you?"

"I saw something."

"Where?" Starsky asked, flicking his gaze around in all directions.

"I mean back in the jail."

Frowning at him, Starsky said, "What are you talking about?"

For a few moments Hutch made no reply, merely sitting with an expression of concentration on his face. Eventually he said, "It's like when Nancy and I were still married, and were going out. When we left the house, she'd always go back, always sure she'd left the water running or something."

"And had she, ever?"

"Usually not. But I have that same feeling about back there. About Fat Rolly. He said something, or did something, that wasn't right. I'm damned if I know what it was. But I saw it. I was there and I saw it."

"Maybe it's like your ex-wife," Starsky said. "You just imagined it."

Chapter 9

As soon as Hutchinson was out of sight, Fat Rolly turned back to the phone and dialed again. When there was an answer, he said, "Sorry I had to hang up. One of the cops who busted me walked up right behind me."

After listening for a few moments, he said without enthusiasm, "Geeze, again? . . . All right, I'll take care of it. Just what's the setup?"

This time there was a long period of listening. Eventually he said, "Got it," and hung up.

When Fat Rolly left Parker Center, he walked along Los Angeles Street two blocks to Third, then stood in front of the window of a secondhand bookstore for five minutes, watching the reflection of every passing vehicle and pedestrian. When he was sure he hadn't been followed, he walked a couple of more blocks along Third, and entered a second-rate hotel.

There was no one on duty at the desk. In lieu of a desk clerk there was a push bell and a sign reading RING BELL FOR SERVICE.

Rolly crossed the dingy lobby to the single elevator and took it to the second floor. Hurrying as fast as his bulk would allow, he waddled to the stairway and descended as far as the landing. From there he could get a view not only of the lobby, but of the front door.

He stood there for several minutes gazing downward, breathing heavily from the exertion of hurrying. He didn't really expect a tail, but he figured that with a pair like Starsky and Hutch, you couldn't be too careful.

When he was satisfied that no one had followed him, he climbed back to the second floor. He found the elevator car still there, its door still open. He got back on and pushed the seventh-floor button.

On seven he went along the hall to a room near the end of the hallway numbered 717. He gave three sharp but widely spaced knocks on the door, then backed across the hall to position himself against the wall directly opposite the peephole in the center of the door. Gazing at the peephole, he smiled a trifle idiotically, like someone posing uncomfortably for a home movie.

Rolly heard the door being unlocked and saw it crack open. He crossed to push it the rest of the way open, went in, and closed and locked it behind him.

The tall, thin man who had opened the door was just reseating himself in a leaking, overstuffed chair facing a television set. The set was black and white, and at the moment a herd of cattle was crossing a Warner Brothers plain. Reading a newspaper on the bed, with his back against a pillow, was a squarely built, powerfully muscled man with blond hair and pale skin.

"Hi, Canelli," the fat man said to the man in the easy chair. He nodded to the one on the bed. " 'Lo, Zale."

The bulky Zale folded his newspaper and regarded Rolly noncommittally. Canelli raised one hand in indifferent greeting without taking his gaze from the television screen.

"One more time," Rolly said.

This got more attention from both men. Both stared

at him. "When?" the thin man asked. "And which?"

"Both together this time," Rolly said. "Tonight. He's getting the dope on where they'll be right now. He wants you to phone in."

Canelli glanced at the phone on the battered dresser.

"From a pay phone," Rolly said.

Giving him an irritated look, the thin man said, "I know." He got to his feet and switched off the television. "I'm never gonna see the end of this goddamned picture," he complained.

Zale swung his feet over the side of the bed and started to put on his shoes.

When Starsky and Hutch left the Parker Center parking lot, Starsky drove along Temple Street. As they passed the Hall of Administration, Hutch said, "You know it's after twelve?"

"Uh-huh. Hungry?"

"I could eat. How about that new health food place over on Wilshire?"

Starsky's expression became pained. "We better go somewhere in the district today."

"Why? We eat in the district every day."

"Give 'em a chance to locate the Torino," Starsky said. "Who the hell would look for us at a health food spot on Wilshire?"

"Hadn't thought of that," Hutch conceded. "May as well start trolling right away."

Starsky turned onto Hope Avenue. "How about Huggy Bear's? Kill two birds with one stone?"

"Only one bird today. He took the boat over to Catalina. I phoned there from the jail. Won't be back until tomorrow morning. I left word we'd be by at eight-thirty sharp."

Starsky emitted a disappointed grunt.

"Doubt he knows the score anyway," Hutch said.

"If he heard there was a contract on us, don't you think he'd have phoned?"

Starsky reflected for a moment. "Yeah, he would have. Must have left for Catalina before the story hit the street. When'd he go?"

"Angie didn't say."

Starsky said, "Huggy Bear's is our best bet for lunch, anyway. Anybody looking for the Torino's bound to check there."

"Okay," Hutch agreed. "Huggy Bear's."

When they reached the café, Starsky parked right in front. Inside they glanced around, saw all the booths were filled, and took stools at the far end of the bar. The pretty black girl tending bar placed cocktail napkins in front of them and gave them a wide smile.

"Surprised to see you, Dianne," Hutch said. "Thought maybe you were the bomb Angie mentioned."

"What bomb?"

"He said Huggy Bear took a bomb along with him to Catalina."

"Oh, *that* bomb. No such luck. Huggy doesn't believe in fooling with the hired help."

"How long's he been gone?" Starsky asked.

"Day before yesterday."

Starsky looked at Hutch. "That explains it. Word hadn't hit the street yet."

Dianne said, "I got a whole bar full of hungry and thirsty customers, fellows. You going to eat or drink?"

"Eat," Hutch said. "Angie knows what I want."

Starsky said, "Yeah, and he never runs out of it, because nobody else will eat it. Liverwurst and onion on rye for me."

As the black girl moved away, Hutch gave Starsky a disapproving look. "You're going to ruin your stomach."

"My stomach knows what it needs," Starsky told him. Feeling in his pockets, he brought out a dime and a nickel and looked at them. "Got a dime?"

"What for?"

"I need a quarter."

Hutch felt in his pockets, produced a dime, and handed it over. Going over to a candy machine near the entrance, Starsky dropped the coins, studied the choices, and pulled one of the levers. He came back to the bar unwrapping a nut chocolate bar.

"You're going to eat that *before* lunch?" Hutch inquired unbelievingly.

"It don't matter whether you eat dessert first or last, Hutch. Everything mixes together in your stomach. Chinese eat dessert first, you know." He took a bite of the candy bar.

"That's an old wives' tale," Hutch told him. "They don't eat dessert at all. They're too smart."

Starsky had finished his candy bar by the time their lunch arrived. As Dianne set the plates before them, she said, "Liverwurst and onion on rye, Starsky. And a steak sandwich for you, Hutch."

"Steak sandwich?" Starsky said, looking at his partner's plate in surprise.

"Made out of soybeans," Dianne explained. "On organic bread. Angie stocks it special for Hutch. Coffee, Starsky?"

"Uh-huh."

She looked at Hutch. "Carrot juice," he said. "Or whatever he's got, if he's out of that."

"Why would he be out of that?" Starsky inquired. "Who the hell else would order it?"

Dianne went to get their beverages. Starsky started to eat his sandwich, avoiding looking at the one his partner was eating. Hutch avoided looking at the liverwurst-and-onion sandwich, too.

When they emerged from Huggy Bear's, the detectives took in the surrounding area on both sides of the street without seeming to be paying particular attention to it, concentrating on the cars parked behind them on this side of the street, but missing nothing on the other side, either.

"No one sitting waiting for us, looks like," Starsky said in a disappointed tone.

"You don't always get a strike on your first trolling run," Hutch said.

Starsky unlocked the car, climbed under the wheel, and reached over to pull up the lock button on the passenger side. Hutch didn't immediately get in, standing for a few moments frowning in the direction behind them.

When he finally got into the car, Starsky asked, "What were you looking at?"

"Car parked back in the next block. Can't be sure, because it's too far away, but I think somebody's sitting in it."

"A tail wouldn't park that far back," Starsky said. "From that distance he couldn't tell which car was pulling out."

"This one he could spot from a half-mile back," Hutch assured him.

Starting the engine, Starsky pulled out from the curb. He kept his eye on the rearview mirror as they cruised slowly for a couple of blocks.

"Nobody on us," he said finally. "Probably some guy waiting for his wife to come out of a store."

They continued to cruise, each as usual missing nothing on his own side of the street. Starsky braked to a halt at a red light.

On the sidewalk on Hutch's side of the street, only a few feet from his open window, there was a wire-mesh refuse basket. Rummaging through it was a lean, bearded, long-haired man in an ankle-length tattered white robe with a rope tied about his waist. Although his matted hair and beard were gray, he appeared to be only in his mid-thirties.

As Hutch watched, the man finished rummaging and gazed with discouragement at the single returnable bottle he had found.

Hutch said, "Didn't get much of a take today, huh, Lijan?"

The man turned burning eyes at him. "Not enough to keep body and soul together."

"Guess a lot of people don't like to think the end of the world is coming," Hutch suggested.

Lijan drew himself up to his full height of about six feet two. "I think it's already happened, brother. And we're all in Hell."

The light changed, and Starsky drove on. In a quizzical tone Hutch said, "Think maybe he's right?"

Starsky was not much given to philosophical introspection, but the concept intrigued him. He said, "He's wrong. It's not Hell, it's a toilet bowl."

Hutch took his eyes from his side of the street long enough to throw his partner a surprised look. "What?"

"This. What we do, where we do it. It's a toilet bowl, and you and I are little bugs trying to crawl out, and every time we get close to the top, somebody starts flushing. You can be thankful that you and me arc two little bugs that know how to swim."

Hutch had turned back to study his side of the street again. He glanced into the sideview mirror on his side, and his eyes narrowed.

"Yeah," he said. "Especially since we got a shark on our tail."

Chapter 10

STARSKY'S LOOK FLASHED to the rearview mirror. Coming up fast behind them was a dark blue New Yorker sedan. He got a glimpse of a broad, pockmarked face above the steering wheel. No one else was in the car.

Hutch opened the glove compartment and took out Starsky's .38 semiautomatic pistol. Tossing it on the seat between them, he leaned forward to slide the rack from under the seat and lift the shotgun onto his lap. Then he tightened his seat belt, braced his feet against the floor where it inclined upward, and nodded to Starsky.

"Here we go," Starsky said.

He floored the accelerator. The car took off with its engine roaring and smoke coming from the back tires. The sudden spurt caught the driver of the New Yorker by surprise, but after a moment he tromped on the accelerator, too.

By then the Torino had a half-block lead, however, and was traveling at sixty miles an hour. Starsky swung around a truck, braked sharply just for a moment before reaching an intersection, then gunned the engine as he careened left around the corner. They made the dirt-track turn with screaming tires.

The trailing New Yorker zoomed around the truck,

too. Its greater bulk forced it to slow considerably more than the Torino in order to maneuver the corner, but its larger engine allowed quicker acceleration on the straightaway, and within moments it was closing in again.

As the Torino's speedometer hovered at seventy, Starsky concentrated his full attention on the road ahead, not even risking a glance at the rearview mirror. Fortunately there was almost no traffic on the street, and what little was moving was coming toward them. That consisted of only two automobiles and a milk truck, and all three pulled over to the right and stopped when they saw the twin cars roaring toward them, just as they would have for a fire engine or ambulance.

Hutch was half turned to look back through the rear window. "He's still there."

Starsky said, "Probably just wants to make friends."

Both cars zipped through an intersection where there were stop signs both ways, not even slowing for them, forcing cars that were beginning to nose through the intersection from both ways on the cross street to screech their brakes. At the next intersection it was a stop street for them only. Starsky geared down, tapped the brakes lightly, and made an even more stomach-churning left turn than the first one.

The New Yorker had closed the interval to only a few car lengths. Not expecting the Torino to attempt a turn at its speed, the driver of the larger car was caught flat-footed. Slamming on the brakes, he attempted to negotiate the turn also, but the car spun out and ended up crosswise in the intersection, the engine stalled.

By the time the driver of the New Yorker restarted the engine, floored the accelerator, and straightened out to shoot after the Torino, it was again screeching left at the end of the block. A car coming up behind the New Yorker halted just as the big car took off, and another coming from the opposite direction pulled over to the right and stopped.

When the New Yorker reached the corner around which the Torino had disappeared, this time the driver maneuvered the turn more carefully. But after rounding the corner, he slammed on the brakes in a panic stop at the sight of the Torino racing directly at him in *reverse*.

Twenty-five feet from the New Yorker, with the pockmarked driver bracing himself for a crash, the Torino, still in reverse, suddenly swung left into a driveway, screeched to a halt, then jumped forward again. Gears popped as Starsky completed the ripping 180-degree turn. He stood on the brakes and brought the Torino to a stop nose to nose with the New Yorker, the two cars no more than a foot apart.

Both doors of the Torino flew open, and Starsky and Hutch came out, running low. They raced either side of the New Yorker, Hutch carrying the shotgun, Starsky gripping his .38 semiautomatic.

The driver raised his hands high, terrified, not about to so much as breathe with the shotgun barrel resting on the bridge of his nose and the pistol muzzle tickling his ear.

Hutch growled, "All right, armpit, who are you and what do you want?"

"Easy, man, easy!" the pockmarked man said in a panicky voice. "Got a message for you, is all."

Starsky said, "What is it?"

"Mr. Tallman would like to meet with you."

Starsky and Hutch looked at each other across the driver. Setting his safety, Starsky shoved his gun under his belt in the middle of his back, beneath the windbreaker. Hutch took the shotgun muzzle from the bridge of the pockmarked man's nose and let the muzzle droop downward. The man cautiously lowered his hands and let out a relieved sigh.

"Why's he want to meet with us?" Hutch asked. "And when?"

"I don't know why," the man said. After a beat, he finished, "But the when is now."

Starsky and Hutch looked at each other again, this time across the roof of the car. "What do you think?" Starsky asked. "Come into my parlor, said the spider to the fly?"

Hutch shook his head. "If he wanted to cream us, he wouldn't invite us over."

"What easier way? He'd figure we'd figure he'd never do it that way, and would be off guard."

Hutch said, "No, he'd figure we'd radio in just where we were going, which we will, and he'd be in the soup if we didn't report back by radio within a reasonable time."

"Then we're going to accept the kind invitation?"

"Why not?" Hutch bent to tell the driver of the New Yorker, "Tell your boss we'll be along."

"Why don't you just follow me?" the driver asked. "I'd have to wait for you to get you in anyway."

Starsky said, "Okay. We'll get out of your way."

A small crowd had gathered on both sidewalks to gawk. As they returned to the car, Starsky called, "Police business, folks. Case of mistaken identity, so there's nothing to see."

The crowd began to disperse.

Back in the car, Starsky backed into the driveway in order to let the New Yorker by, then followed. Hutch stowed away the shotgun, then removed his little Beretta and both shoulder harnesses from the glove compartment. Dropping the harness for the .38 on the seat, he slipped out of his sport jacket, put on his harness, slipped his gun into it, and put his jacket back on.

Glancing down at his own harness, Starsky said, "Can't put it on while I'm driving."

"Suppose we'll stop eventually," Hutch said.

He brought out the microphone from under the dashboard and pressed the transmit button. "Cruiser Three to Control One. Come in, Control One."

A voice from the radio said, "Control One here, Cruiser Three."

Hutch said, "We've been invited to visit Mr. Gerald Tallman. We're following a guide car to his place now. We have no idea what he wants, but if we don't check back in within, say, an hour and a half, you might send a few cops to break down the door to his penthouse apartment."

"Gerald Tallman, the racketeer?" the radio voice inquired.

"Right."

"Aren't you guys witnesses against him in his upcoming trial?"

"Right again," Hutch said.

"You think it wise to accept his invitation?"

"If we were wise, we wouldn't be cops," Hutch said. "You're just supposed to dispatch and take messages, Control One, not give advice. Over and out."

"Okay, Cruiser Three," the dispatcher said. "Over and out too."

Hutch hung up the microphone.

The New Yorker led them to West Los Angeles and down into the underground garage beneath a seventeen-story apartment building. The pockmarked driver pulled into a slot and motioned Starsky to pull into the vacant slot next to him.

Getting out of the car, but leaving the door open, Starsky stripped off his windbreaker, dropped it on the seat, and slipped on his shoulder harness. He put the windbreaker back on before transferring his gun from behind him under his belt to his shoulder holster. The pockmarked man stood with Hutch and waited patiently while this was taking place.

When Starsky was ready and had locked the Torino, the driver led the way over to an elevator. An indicator showed the car was on the first floor. The driver pushed the call button to bring it down. When they got on, he pushed the button marked "17."

"You got a name?" Starsky asked the man.

"Melvin."

"A last name, too?" Hutch asked.

After considering the question, Melvin shrugged and said, "Smith."

When they reached the seventeenth floor, Melvin led the way across the hall to another elevator with a narrow door, about the width of an ordinary room door. This one he unlocked with a key. The detectives noted that the control panel in the closet-sized car had only two buttons, one marked "U" and the other marked "D." Melvin pushed the "U" button.

The car rose one flight to the penthouse apartment. The elevator door gave onto a small entryway, but when the door opened, they couldn't get off, because a steel grille barred the way. A large redheaded man in an expensive suit stood on the other side of the grille, looking in at them.

"Detectives Starsky and Hutchinson, Carl," Melvin said.

Nodding, the oversized Carl released a catch and slid open the steel grille. He crossed the entryway to the door leading into the apartment, paused with his hand on the knob, and said over his shoulder in a guttural voice that made him sound like Marlon Brando with tissue paper stuffed in his cheeks, "You guys heeled?"

"Thoroughly," Hutch assured him.

76

Carl looked thoughtful, then shrugged. "We'll talk about that later."

He opened the door and led the way into the apartment's front room. The instant effect was stunning. Aside from being an enormous room furnished expensively and in exquisite taste, both side walls were of floor-to-ceiling glass, giving a view of the city from horizon to horizon. But the most stunning part was the personnel occupying the room.

Another large man, this one black, went barely noticed by the two detectives. He was seated in an easy chair next to one transparent wall, reading a newspaper. What monopolized their attention were the four women standing in various parts of the room. All were in their twenties, all wore simple hostess gowns of differing colors, very low-cut, and all were beautiful. There was a black girl in bright red, an oriental girl in green, an American Indian girl in white, and a platinum blond in pink.

The black girl came over, showed small, perfect white teeth in a smile, and said, "Detectives Starsky and Hutchinson?"

Both nodded.

"I'm Maxine, the maid," she said, making a slight curtsy.

Starsky tore his gaze from her cleavage to look at the other girls. "All maids?" he asked.

"Yes," Maxine said brightly. "There are a lot of rooms to take care of here. This way, please."

She preceded them through a door at the far end of the room. As they passed the other maids, the girls all threw them smiles. Starsky and Hutch smiled back.

The black bodyguard threw his paper aside and got up from his chair. He and the redheaded bodyguard followed along.

The procession went down a long hall, past a number of doors, and finally turned into a huge bedroom.

Pointing to the bed, the beautiful black girl said, "You may lay them there."

"Lay what there?" Hutch asked.

"Your things. Take off your clothes, please."

Chapter 11

HUTCH AND STARSKY LOOKED at the girl steadily for a few moments, looked from her to the two bodyguards, and then at each other.

Finally looking back at Maxine, Hutch said, "Uh—why do we have to take off our clothes?"

"Because Mr. Tallman is in the sauna and he expects you to join him there."

Starsky and Hutch looked at each other again, weighing the matter.

In his godfather voice, the big redheaded bodyguard said, "See, if you got your clothes off, Mr. Tallman knows you ain't heeled, and that you're not wired for sound. Mr. Tallman don't like people what are wired for sound."

Hutch said, "There goes his invitation to San Clemente."

The redhead started to reach under Starsky's windbreaker for his .38, at the same time saying, "So, if you don't mind, we'll just—."

That was as far as he got when Starsky indicated that he did mind by swiftly raising a knee into the bodyguard's crotch. The man fell to his knees, doubled over, emitting whinnying little groans. The black bodyguard took a step toward Starsky, but halted when he found himself looking down the barrel of the .38.

When he stepped back again, Starsky lowered the gun muzzle.

After a time the oversized redhead stopped making distressed noises, painfully climbed to his feet, and glared at Starsky. Starsky said, "It's not polite to reach, Carl," flipped the weapon in his hand, and held it out butt first.

Taking the gun, Carl continued to glare at Starsky murderously, his thumb caressing the safety catch, as though he were seriously considering shooting him.

Ignoring him, Starsky said to the maid in an offhand tone, "This isn't likely to take more than an hour, is it?"

"I have no idea," she said. "Why? Do you have an appointment?"

"Not exactly. It's just that we radioed in to have a rescue squad beat down your front door if we didn't call in again within an hour and a half. And that was about a half-hour ago."

"I'll make sure to buzz the sauna in forty-five minutes," Maxine said.

The black bodyguard had been looking inquiringly at Hutch, not about to make the same mistake his partner had. Hutch took out his Beretta and tossed it to him. He dropped it into his pocket, and after glowering at Starsky for a moment more, the red-haired man shoved the .38 into his coat pocket.

Starsky took off his windbreaker, tossed it onto the bed, and tossed his shoulder harness on top of it. Hutch threw his sport jacket and his harness next to Starsky's stuff. Then both looked at the black girl.

"You just going to stand there and watch?" Starsky asked.

"I have to show you to the sauna."

Starsky and Hutch looked at each other, then both shrugged. Then continued to strip.

As he folded his slacks and draped them across the

bed, Hutch said, "My mother always used to tell me to wear clean underwear in case I was ever in an accident. Didn't want me to shock the nurses." After a pause, he added, "This particular situation didn't enter into the conversation, as I recall."

Starsky said, "My mother always yapped at me if I put on torn underwear, for the same reason. I'd tell her not to worry, because if I ended up in the hospital, the nurses would think it got torn in the accident." Tossing his trousers on the bed, he looked down at himself and said, "Guess what? I've got a tear in my shorts."

"I won't tell your mother," Maxine said dryly.

When both detectives were stripped, the bodyguards left the room, presumably feeling that their nakedness reduced the pair to harmlessness.

Maxine led the way out of the room and down the hall.

Opening a door, she showed them into a small room containing a sofa, a couple of overstuffed leather chairs, and a cocktail table. In a little alcove off to the side, two doors faced each other. One led into a shower. The other, of heavy cedar, with a small glass window in it, was obviously to the sauna bath.

Sliding back the wooden panel of a built-in cabinet, the black girl took out two large towels and handed one to each detective. "Either of you like anything to drink?" she asked.

"We're on duty," Hutch said.

Her gaze briefly flicked to below his waist. With a wide smile she said, "Couldn't tell, honey. You ain't wearing no badge."

She left the room.

Starsky led the way over to the door of the sauna, opened it, and went in with Hutch right behind him. It was a unique sauna bath. Instead of the usual dim lighting by a single low-watt bulb, the little room was brightly illuminated by sunlight. The walls on either side were the customary cedar, with cedar benches running along them, but the wall opposite the door was of thick glass, giving a view of the city spreading off into the distance.

Seated on a towel on the cedar bench to the right was a man of around sixty, gray-haired and tall and thin, with sunken cheekbones and a wasted figure that showed evidence of once having been muscular. But despite his appearance of failing health, there was an air of command about him, like that of an aging general whose exercise of authority is undiminished by approaching old age.

Smiling at Starsky and Hutch, he gestured toward the bench facing his. But both officers first walked over to look at the breathtaking view through the glass wall.

"Pretty, isn't it?" Gerald Tallman said.

Starsky and Hutch merely nodded, continuing to take in the view.

Tallman said sardonically, "Crime *does* pay, you see."

Hutch turned to the cedar bench facing the racketeer, spread his towel on it, and sat down. Starsky sat to his partner's left.

Hutch said, "Does it pay enough to make you want to kill us?"

In a dismissing tone, Tallman said, "No. But crime creates wealth, wealth begets envy, and someone who envies me is attempting to frame me with your murders."

Starsky said, "We haven't been murdered yet, so you're in the clear."

"I know, but they'll try again. Sometime today or tomorrow, or tomorrow night. No later."

"How do you figure that?" Hutch asked.

"Because the trial is set for the day after tomorrow, and you two are scheduled as the first two prosecution witnesses. If they kill you after that, I'll have no motive, and they can't frame me. That's really what this is all about."

Hutch raised a quizzical eyebrow. "In other words, we'll be dead, but you'll be the injured party."

The racketeer nodded. "Exactly."

Hutch said argumentatively, "But you know damn well if we both get to court and testify, you're nailed with a very heavy fall."

"Not really. Let me tell you how it will work. If you testify, I'll be found guilty because, as we all know, I am guilty. Then my lawyers will ask the judge to set bail, which will be an outrageous sum, but not so outrageous that I can't pay it, and so I'll be home in time for cocktails. Then my lawyers will appeal, and the appeal will be denied, and then they'll appeal higher up, and that appeal will be denied, and eventually it will have been kept in the courts for five or six years. Now, I'm sixty-one and have pernicious anemia. My father died at fifty-eight of the same disease. By actuarial projections, I'll never make it to sixty-five, so the courts will end up finding me guilty two years after I'm dead." His tone became mildly sardonic. "I think I'll be able to weather the disgrace of it all. Would you like a drink?"

Both detectives shook their heads, only partly in refusal of the invitation, and primarily in wonderment at the reasoned calmness with which the racketeer viewed the trial ahead of him. Exchanging glances, they tacitly agreed that his assessment of the outcome was very probably accurate.

Looking back at Tallman, Starsky said, "Okay. So you want to help us stay alive so you don't get framed?"

"If I can."

"You probably can," Starsky assured him. "Do you

know a team, two guys, that works at pointblank range with sawed-off shotguns?"

"Yes, I do. But the two men I know wouldn't have made the mistake those two made, killing the wrong people."

"What are their names?"

Tallman shook his head. "I'm not going to give you their names. They didn't do it. If they had, you'd be dead."

Starsky frowned. "You're sure of that?"

"Absolutely certain. I have a suggestion. Why don't you stay over here for the next couple of days? You will be royally entertained, I assure you. Then we could all leave for the trial together, and there's no way I could be blamed for your murders."

Starsky looked at Hutch, a wistful expression in his eyes, thinking of the four beautiful maids, but resigned to the fact that it was impossible to accept the invitation.

Hutch confirmed that by saying, "We have appointments."

"Are those appointments worth dying for?" Tallman inquired.

That was a question they dealt with daily. Both men shrugged. Starsky said laconically, "Even dying's a living."

Tallman sighed. "I assume you will report this conference to your immediate superior. Captain Dobey, isn't it?"

Both men nodded. Hutch said, "We generally keep him informed of what's going on."

"Then at least it will be on record that you agree I have no real motive for putting out a contract on you two. Then if—"

When he let it trail off, Hutch said softly, "Then if we're hit, you've got it both ways. The bribery case collapses for lack of witnesses, and you're also off the hook for our murders."

Tallman frowned. "Come, come, Officer Hutchinson," he said chidingly. "I'm not that Machiavellian."

"We think you are," Starsky said bluntly.

Hutch said, "That may not be your devious plan, but we wouldn't put it past you. Just in case you are that Machiavellian, Starsky and I aren't going to mention this meeting to a soul until after the trial. That will give you some incentive to see that we manage to stay alive at least that long. Might induce you to let us know anything you hear, or even to set some of your boys to inquiring around."

Something approaching admiration briefly appeared in the older man's eyes. "You're a little Machiavellian yourselves. In self-defense I might just do that. I'm obliged for the suggestion."

Rising to his feet, Starsky said, "I've had enough. Baking, I mean, not the company. Thanks for the sauna."

"Anytime," Tallman said courteously. "Please come back sometime for a purely social visit."

Hutch said regretfully, "The chief frowns on cops mixing socially with known racketeers. But thanks for the invitation."

They left the sauna, showered, and walked back up hall to the bedroom where they had left their clothing.

As they started to dress, Starsky asked, "Suppose it would be ethical to accept his protection for just about an hour?"

Glancing at his watch, Hutch said, "We would only get interrupted. Cops are going to start axing the door down if we don't radio in before another twenty minutes."

They had just finished dressing when Maxine appeared in the bedroom doorway.

"Oh, there you are," she said. "I was heading for the sauna to remind you of the time."

She continued along the hall in the direction of the sauna.

Starsky and Hutch went the other way, into the front room. The three other maids, the two bodyguards, and the driver of the New Yorker were all still there. The girls all smiled at the detectives, and Starsky and Hutch smiled back. Starsky held out his hand to the red-haired bodyguard, and Hutch held his out to the black man.

"Not just yet," the redhead said.

"Why not?" Starsky inquired with a frown.

"Soon as Maxine gets back."

It was obvious the black girl was checking to make sure Tallman had been left unharmed before they would be allowed to leave. Starsky and Hutch could hardly resent the precaution.

A few moments later Maxine reappeared. When she nodded to the two bodyguards, the detective's guns were handed back to them.

The pockmarked Melvin accompanied them to the seventeenth floor on the penthouse elevator, but then left them to take the other elevator the rest of the way down by themselves.

Chapter 12

As THEY WAITED for the main elevator, Starsky said regretfully, "To bad we had to refuse that nice invitation."

"Aside from the ethics involved, I can think of two reasons to refuse," Hutch told him. "First, we've got that narcotics stakeout all set up for tonight."

"What's the other?"

"I've got a date afterward."

Starsky stared at him. "That stakeout may last till three A.M."

"Doesn't matter. She isn't coming in until midnight. And she knows where the key is."

"Coming in from where?"

"Chicago, I think. Or maybe St. Louis. Airline stewardess."

"Oh. Ginger."

Hutch shook his head.

"Gwen?"

Hutch shook his head again.

"Well, who?" Starsky asked, exasperated.

"A new one you haven't met. Molly."

The elevator door opened, and they got on. They had no further conversation on the way down to the basement garage, both concentrating on the blinking floor indicator. When the "1" blinked out, and just before "B" lit up, both moved over in front of the door, side by side, prepared to step off as soon as the door opened.

A black sedan was parked in the driving lane directly in front of the elevator, no more than a dozen feet away, facing the exit ramp. Hutch didn't see it, because he had just turned his head toward Starsky to say something to him. But Starsky happened to be looking straight ahead.

In the brief instant after the door opened, Starsky didn't see the car well enough even to note its make, because his attention was riveted on the four shotgun barrels pointing their way. He didn't even see the faces of the two men leaning on their elbows across the hood of the car, because he reacted before he had time to look at *anything* other than the gun muzzles.

Both of Starsky's palms hit Hutch's left shoulder, stiff-arming him to one side of the door at the same time Starsky threw himself to the other side. The roar that followed was deafening in the confines of the low-ceilinged basement garage. The four loads of buckshot hit the rear elevator wall with the sound of a giant spade smacking against a tin roof. The wall buckled and several cracks appeared in it.

If the pellets had been steel instead of lead, the ricochets probably would have killed both detectives. As it was, they merely flattened and fell to the floor.

Apparently the blast damaged the elevator's electrical wiring system, because the light in the ceiling went out and the door slammed shut. On the other side of the door they heard the sedan roar up the exit ramp.

"You all right, Hutch?" Starsky asked into the darkness.

"Oh, sure," Hutch said nonchalantly. "I have nerves of steel." After a pause, he appended, "Twan-n-ng!"

Starsky felt for the door, pressed both palms against

it and pushed sideways. It opened a crack. Hutch, his Beretta in his hand, put his eye to the crack. There was no one within his range of vision, which was what he had expected after hearing the car roar up the exit ramp, but he wasn't rash enough to place complete faith in his hearing.

Satisfied that there was no immediate danger on the other side of the door, he put away his gun, gripped the door with both hands, and heaved. When it opened a couple of feet, he put his shoulder against it and forced it the rest of the way open.

As he and Starsky stepped out, the door slammed closed again.

"Why did it do that with the electricity off?" Starsky asked curiously.

"I don't know, but I'm not going to take the time to find out," Hutch said. "Let's get moving."

Both men ran to the Torino. Starsky unlocked the car, slid under the wheel, and unlocked Hutch's side. He had the engine started by the time Hutch slammed his door.

As they emerged onto the street, their gazes instantly took in everything in both directions. There was no sign of the black sedan. Starsky swung in the direction of Wilshire Boulevard.

Hutch hit the transmit button of the microphone and said, "Cruiser Three to Control One. Come in, Control One."

The voice of the radio dispatcher sounded relieved. "Welcome back, Cruiser Three. We were starting to get antsy around here about you. What is your location?"

"Just leaving the apartment building where Tallman lives, heading toward Wilshire to return to the district. We want an APB on a car somewhere in this area with two men in it armed with sawed-off double-barreled shotguns." He looked at Starsky and released the transmit button. "You get any kind of a look at them?"

Taking the mike from him, Starsky said into it, "Still Cruiser Three here. The shotgunners are in a black sedan, make unknown, but fairly new. Can't describe the two men, but they're probably the same ones who blew apart those two kids in the Torino last night. They just tried to blow us apart. Over."

"Tried to blow you apart where, Cruiser Three?" the radio voice asked.

Hutch said into the microphone, "As we were getting off the elevator in the basement garage after coming down from Tallman's penthouse. Put the elevator out of commission, but didn't hurt either of us."

"Tallman guns?" the dispatcher asked.

"Don't think so," Hutch said. "He wouldn't have it pulled there. Too raw. Any messages?"

"Negative, Cruiser Three. I'll get out an APB, but don't expect any miracles with that vague description."

"We won't," Hutch said. "Cruiser Three over and out."

As he hung up the microphone, he said, "You didn't see much, considering you were looking right at them."

"I was concentrating on the shotgun bores," Starsky said. "The smaller the gauge, the bigger the bore, is the way it works, isn't it? I mean a ten-gauge is bigger than a twelve-gauge, isn't it?"

"Uh-huh."

"Those had to be one-gauge," Starsky said.

Without taking his gaze from his side of the street, Hutch grinned. "If there were such a thing, it would be about the size of a ninety-millimeter cannon."

"That was the size," Starsky said positively. "Incidentally, you're welcome."

"For saving my life?" Hutch said. "Chalk it up against the two times I've saved yours. But thanks anyway."

They reached Wilshire and Starsky turned east. Glancing at his watch, he said, "You know it's three o'clock?"

"So?"

"So maybe we better log out soon as we get back. We've got that stakeout tonight, and you know how Dobey screams if we log too much overtime."

"Point well taken," Hutch said. "I ought to get in a nap and take some vitamins anyway, so as to be up to par tonight."

"For the stakeout?"

"No, for afterward."

As they pulled onto the parking lot at Vinnie's Gym, Hutch lifted the microphone again. "Cruiser Three to Control One. Come in, Control One."

"Control One," the radio said. "Go ahead, Cruiser Three."

Looking at his watch, Hutch said, "Log us out at three-twenty."

"Okay, Cruiser Three. Little early, though, isn't it?"

"We have to log back in for stakeout duty tonight," Hutch said. "Cruiser Three over and out."

Starsky had pulled the Torino in next to Hutch's brown Ford. As Hutch got out of the car, Starsky said, "Pick you up about nine-thirty?"

"Little late, isn't it?" Hutch said.

"We don't have to relieve Landau and Newcombe until ten."

"Okay," Hutch said. "That crate ought to be able to make it from Venice to Hollywood in a half-hour."

He climbed into his own car. Starsky waved to him, swung around, and drove off the lot toward home.

Promptly at nine-thirty Starsky pulled the Torino in next to Hutch's little canal-side cottage in Venice. The small one-story building, surrounded by a white picket fence whose front was almost on the edge of the canal, was a picture-postcard spot. Starsky was sometimes tempted to get something like it for himself, but he wouldn't have been happy in suburbia, or anywhere other than in a midcity apartment.

A tap on the horn brought Hutch from the cottage. Locking the door behind him, he put the key under a flowerpot just inside the gate.

As Hutch got into the car, Starsky lifted the microphone and called Control One. "Log us in at nine-thirty. We're leaving Sergeant Hutchinson's house in Venice en route to the Palm Street stakeout in Hollywood."

"Roger, Cruiser Three," the dispatcher said. "You're logged in."

"Cruiser Three over and out."

At about that time Fat Rolly was again giving the code knock on the door of room 717 at the hotel on Third Street in downtown Los Angeles. When he had been studied through the peephole and admitted to the room, he found Canelli and Zale in the same positions as last time, Canelli watching television from the worn easy chair, Zale seated on the bed with a pillow behind his back.

Rolly was more assured than on his previous visit. "The Man wants an encore."

The pale-skinned Zale regarded him somberly. "He had an encore. How many's he want?"

"This probably will be the last."

Canelli turned to give him an irritated look. "It better be, fat man."

Rolly stared at him resentfully, but when Canelli gave him a baleful look back, he averted his eyes. "You got a real good chance tonight," he said. "They'll be all alone in a dark spot, wide open."

"Where and when?" Zale asked.

"Narcotics stakeout in Hollywood. I'll show you on a city map."

Taking an Automobile Club map of Los Angeles from his pocket, he spread it on top of the battered dresser. Canelli and Zale both rose to come over and look at the map.

When Fat Rolly left fifteen minutes later, the two hit men dressed to go out, putting on dark clothing and hats that pulled down over their eyes. They got off the elevator in the basement garage of the hotel a few minutes later, black leather clarinet-sized cases in hand. They set them on the back floor of the black sedan parked near the exit ramp.

This time the muscular Zale got behind the wheel, and the thin man took the passenger seat. The car moved up the ramp to the street.

Directly across the street from the garage exit was a phone booth. Inside, with the door open so that the ceiling bulb would not go on and he could remain invisible in the darkness, stood Fat Rolly, who had been waiting there ever since he left the hotel. As soon as the black sedan drove off, Rolly closed the door and dialed a number.

The phone rang only once before it was answered.

"Rolly here," the fat man said. "They're on their way, sir."

Chapter 13

THE APARTMENT COMPLEX on Palm Street was large and expensive. Eight stories tall, it was U-shaped, with the bottom of the U toward the street. An archway in front led into a courtyard a good fifty yards square, centered by a swimming pool. Chaises longues surrounded the swimming pool, and a number of stone benches edged the curving walks. There were a lot of ferns, small palm trees, rubber trees, buses, and a few banana trees planted in haphazard order.

The entrances to the apartments were all outdoors, and all faced the inner courtyard. Those above ground level gave onto railed balconies overlooking the courtyard. There was an elevator with an outside door in each corner of the courtyard.

There were parking lots on either side of the building, but signs over the entrances read PARKING FOR TENANTS ONLY—UNAUTHORIZED VEHICLES WILL BE TOWED AWAY AT OWNERS' EXPENSE. Starsky drove onto one of the lots anyway, but when he found all the slots were numbered and most were filled, he drove off again. He finally found a parking place on the street a block away.

It was just ten P.M. when Starsky and Hutch walked through the archway into the courtyard. The lighted swimming pool cast enough of a glow for them to see the central part of the courtyard clearly, although its edges were draped in shadow. It was too cool a night for swimming, and no one was in sight.

As the two detectives stood looking around, the swimming pool lights suddenly were doused, leaving the courtyard in pitch darkness except for what light came from apartment windows—and that wasn't much, because most had drawn drapes.

"Must turn the lights off at ten o'clock," Hutch said. He hunched his shoulders. "Wish I'd worn a warmer jacket. How can it get this cold in May?"

Starsky, who had worn a woolen zippered jacket, said, "I don't feel cold. Where do you suppose Landau and Newcombe are?"

"Somewhere in the bushes. They must have seen us before the lights went out. Let's stay put and let them come to us."

A few moment later dim figures approached from each direction. Both were middle-aged men, dressed in dark clothing.

"Right on time," Detective Lou Landau said. "That warm bed's gonna feel good."

"Anything going on?" Starsky asked.

Don Newcombe said, "Nope. We got here at six o'clock. He's been in his apartment. Hasn't budged."

"Which place is it?" Starsky asked.

"Come on back by the swimming pool," Landau said, leading the way.

When all four detectives were gathered at the far end of the pool, Landau pointed upward. "That lighted room with its drapes open on the top floor. Directly over the archway."

Gazing at the indicated windows, both Starsky and Hutch nodded. Hutch asked, "He got the stuff up there?"

"We think so," Landau said. "We can't prove it, or

even show enough cause to get a warrant, but we think it's there."

"We've got to nail him with it, then?" Starsky said.

"That's it," Landau said. "If there's going to be a buy, you're the boys to handle it."

Hutch said a trifle dryly, "We aren't boys."

After looking at him for a moment, Landau smiled slightly. "Neither are the guys you're trying to nail," he said with equal dryness. "Take care."

He and his partner moved off in the darkness toward the archway.

Looking up at the lighted windows again, Starsky said, "Right in the middle, you could take either elevator to get there."

"Yeah," Hutch agreed. "We better split and cover both."

"I'll take right," Starsky said, jerking a thumb in that direction.

He moved off that way, and Hutch moved in the opposite direction. Starsky found a spot about twenty feet from the elevator on his side, where a bush and a huge fern formed a concealing pocket just big enough to sit in. Settling himself, he took a small citizen's band radio from his pocket, pushed the transmit button, and said, "Testing. You set, Hutch?"

After a short wait, Hutch's voice said, "I guess. This ground is damn cold."

"Think there's really any stuff up there?" Starsky asked.

Hutch said, "Enough cocaine to float the *Andrea Doria,* probably. Hey, look up."

A distinguished-looking older man in a sporty jacket had stepped from the door of the staked-out apartment, a drink in his hand. Walking over to the eighth-floor railing, he gazed down into the courtyard.

"Fleming?" Starsky asked.

"That's our hero. Looks like somebody's kindly uncle, doesn't he, the sonovabitch."

"Tsk, tsk," Starsky said reprovingly. "Just because he deals cocaine to eleven-year-old kids is no reason for disrespect to your elders. Looks like he's waiting for somebody."

"Well, so are we," Hutch said.

The distinguished-looking man took a sip of his drink, peered down into the courtyard again, then returned to his apartment. There was a long wait.

After about fifteen minutes, Hutch, seated in the shadow of a large bush with his back against a banana tree, said into the radio, "Jesus, it's getting cold."

"Think about your friend Molly?" Starsky's voice advised.

A woman's laughter, throaty, full of enjoyment, came floating down from one of the upper stories. Hutch searched the upper reaches, trying to guess its source, then said into the radio, "Hey, Starsky, that came from seven, about halfway between the archway and your elevator. The place where a light's on behind the drawn drapes, and a window's cracked open."

After a wait, Starsky's voice said, "See it. Sounds like a redhead. About twenty-three."

"How much you can deduce from just a laugh, Holmes," Hutch said with mock admiration. "Tell us what she's laughing at?"

"Old Laurel and Hardy movie, probably."

Another burst of laughter came from above, this time containing a note of uncontrol, as though the woman were being held down and tickled.

Hutch said dryly, "Yeah, I guess I forgot how funny Laurel and Hardy are."

The slim figure of a man was briefly silhouetted in the archway by the light from the street. He turned left, in Starsky's direction, before the concealed detectives could get more than a momentary glimpse of him.

"See that guy?" Hutch asked over the radio.

"Yeah," Starsky said. "Think it was Dallaway?"

"Too dark, but it was his build."

In a lower tone, almost a whisper, Starsky said, "Here he comes. By the elevator. It's Dallaway, all right. He's not twenty feet from me."

"Then you better shut up, or he'll hear you," Hutch said.

The elevator was on an upper floor and had to be brought down. Starsky got an even better look at the man when the door opened, because the car was lighted. He was in his mid-twenties, wore conservative but expensively tailored clothing, and had a styled haircut. He looked like a junior executive for some large corporation.

The young man took the elevator to the eighth floor and walked along the balcony to the apartment from which the distinguished-looking man had emerged. As he knocked on the door, Starsky set down his radio and took a small but powerful set of binoculars from his jacket pocket. He focused them on the eighth-floor apartment door.

The door was opened by the distinguished-looking man. The younger man took a banded sheaf of currency from his inside breast pocket and handed it to him. The older man smiled, said something and closed the door. The youthful Dallaway started back toward the elevator.

Replacing the binoculars in his pocket, Starsky picked up the radio. "Have the glasses on 'em?" he asked.

"Uh-huh," Hutch's voice said.

"See Fleming pass him anything?"

"I saw him *not* pass him anything. Definitely."

"As usual," Starsky said in a depressed tone. "Think we ought to shake Dallaway down anyway?"

"No. He's never had it on him before, so there's no reason to think he's carrying it now."

"Then how are they getting the junk out?"

"Patience, patience," Hutch said. "And you better shut up again. The elevator's almost down."

The elevator door opened, and the young dope dealer stepped out. It seemed to Starsky that there was a smug expression on his face, but it may have been his imagination. Dallaway returned to the archway and exited through it.

"Now what?" Starsky inquired into the radio.

"We wait," Hutch's voice came back.

They waited for fifteen minutes. Then the lights in the eighth-floor apartment went out.

"Cripes," Starsky said into the radio. "He's going to bed."

"Looks like it," Hutch agreed glumly. Then his voice picked up. "Hey, wait a minute. He's on the balcony."

Peering upward, Starsky made out a dim figure standing by the railing in front of the apartment. He was reaching for his binoculars when some kind of object arched out from the figure to fall eight stories and splash into the deep end of the swimming pool. Then the figure disappeared into the apartment.

"What was that?" Starsky asked into the radio.

"Package about the size of a shoe box," Hutch's voice came back. "I got my glasses on it just as he threw it."

"What d'ya think?"

"Beats the hell out of me," Hutch said. "We wait some more, I guess."

"Not very long," Starsky said. "Check the high diving board."

Hutch had to come to his feet and move a few paces from the banana tree in order to see the diving board, because the bush that had been concealing him was in the way. A figure all in black and wearing black tennis shoes was climbing down the ladder from the twelve-foot-high platform of the high diving board.

Starsky said, "Must be the third one, Mooney. No wonder he never comes along with his partner when Dallaway makes a buy. While we're covering Dallaway, Mooney sneaks in the back way and waits to pick up the stuff. Cute."

Hutch said, "He must have walked in from the alley and climbed up there after we got in position. Right under our noses. Shall we take him?"

"Not until he recovers the stuff," Starsky said. "We have to take him with it in his actual possession. But we can move in closer."

The man in black reached the bottom of the ladder and lifted a long pole with a lifesaving hook on the end from which it hung on the diving board tower. He began to fish along the bottom of the pool with it.

Out in front of the apartment complex a dark sedan pulled into the no-parking zone directly opposite the archway. Zale and Canelli reached onto the floor in back, lifted their black leather cases, and set them on their laps. Taking out the double-barreled sawed-off shotguns, they set the cases between them on the front seat and broke the guns to make sure they were loaded.

As they snapped them closed again, Zale said, "Hey."

"What?" his partner asked.

"End of the picture, Montgomery Clift knocks John Wayne on his tail, and Wayne decides the kid's tough enough to be his partner."

Canelli said petulantly, "I asked you not to tell me."

"Let's go," Zale said, and climbed from the car.

Canelli got out the other side. After glancing around in all directions, they walked side by side toward the archway, their guns held muzzle down next to their right legs.

Chapter 14

STARSKY AND HUTCH moved in cautiously from opposite directions to within about twenty feet of the pool, Starsky finally halting behind a thick palm tree, Hutch crouching behind a large fern. From that distance they could make out the dark-clothed figure a little better, although not clearly. He was a muscular man in his thirties, wearing a black turtleneck sweater and black slacks.

The man's probing with the lifesaving hook stopped, and he lifted the pole from the water. Dangling from its end was a plastic-wrapped shoe box with a cord tied around the center and a loop formed in the cord at the top of the box. The hook was through the loop.

Unhooking the box, the man hung up the pole and started along the edge of the pool on Starsky's side in the direction of the alley.

Starsky and Hutch both burst from their hiding places. Aiming his Beretta, Hutch called out, "Police officer! Freeze!"

The order merely caused the man in black to break into a run, clutching the shoe box to his chest like a football. He wasn't aware that there was another police officer in addition to the one who had challenged him until Starsky charged into him, driving him over the pool edge into the shallow end, and following right along with him. The box flew across the pool, landing on the top of the underwater steps at the shallow end on Hutch's side, no more than a foot below the surface.

The man in black surged to his feet and took a wild swing at Starsky. Blocking it, Starsky grabbed his wrist, spun him around with his arm twisted up into the center of his back, and began to force him through the waist-high water toward Hutch's side of the pool.

Hutch, his Beretta in his right hand, held out his left to grip the man's left and help him from the pool. Starsky, figuring the gun in his partner's hand was enough to keep the suspect under control, released his grip on the man's wrist. Hutch pulled him up to a kneeling position on the edge of the pool, released his hand, and stepped back to cover him with his pistol.

As Hutch straightened, he became aware from the corner of his vision of two figures coming through the archway. He turned his head toward the twin silhouettes, one tall and thin, the other squarely built, just in time to see them bring up the sawed-off shotguns.

There wasn't time to shout a warning. Hutch dived headfirst at Starsky, his outstretched left hand catching his partner in the chest and driving him over on his back. As both went under, the four barrels of the shotguns roared, echoing back and forth between the walls of the courtyard.

The man in black, just rising to his feet, was blasted back into the pool again. Starsky and Hutch surfaced, Starsky sputtering, and crouched with just their heads out of the water, looking toward the archway. It was now empty, except for a thick cloud of gun smoke still hanging in the air.

The two detectives got to their feet and sloshed toward the shallow-end steps, barely glancing at the dead man floating on his back nearby. Hutch already had his Beretta in his hand. Starsky drew his .38. Hutch grabbed up the plastic-coated box as he went up the steps.

Then they were running toward the archway in their waterlogged clothing. A black sedan without lights pulled out of the no-parking place in front as they reached the inner edge of the archway. It was at the intersection a half-block away and was swinging left by the time they got to the outer edge.

Starsky and Hutch looked at each other, put away their guns, and shrugged. Hutch said dourly, "Glad you found a parking place close by. Makes it handy to get to the radio."

Starsky made no reply. They walked back through the archway, dripping. Lights had gone on all over the building, and people were emerging into the courtyard from the first-floor apartments and were crowding the balconies above.

The pool lights suddenly went on, not only illuminating the area, but giving those on the balconies a view of the body floating face up in the pool with wide-staring eyes, and with reddened water all around it. Gasps came from a hundred throats.

Starsky boomed in a voice loud enough to carry to the top balcony, "Police officers! We want this courtyard cleared. You first-floor people get back in your apartments."

A number of residents had been inching toward the pool, but Starsky's authoritative tone stopped them. After some hesitation, everyone filed back inside, but doors remained open and drapes were pulled back so that they could view what was going on.

Glancing around, Starsky saw a doorway just to the left of the archway with a sign over it reading MANA-GER. A plump, middle-aged man wearing a robe over pajamas stood in the open doorway. An equally plump woman in a robe was staring out the window.

Starsky said to the man, "You the manager?"

"Yes, sir."

"Go call the police, please. Tell them Starsky and Hutchinson want a Homicide team here right away."

"Yes, sir," the man said, going inside and closing the door.

Starsky and Hutch went on to the pool edge. Looking down at the floating body, Hutch said, "Poor Mooney. Never knew what hit him."

Turning, he glanced upward toward the eighth floor. Seeing him look that way, Starsky looked up, too. The distinguished-looking man, now wearing a robe over pajamas, was among those gazing down at the pool. When he saw the detectives looking at him, he turned and reentered his apartment.

"Does us seeing him toss the stuff in the pool constitute reasonable cause for search and seizure without a warrant?" Starsky asked.

Hutch shook his head. "Never hold, because so far it's just a shoe box. We haven't had the contents analyzed." After a pause, he added, "Besides, he's gonna have everything else he has on hand flushed down the toilet before we could ever get up there."

Starsky grunted. "Let's go see if that manager has some way to get our clothes dry. I'm freezing."

"You're freezing?" Hutch said with a shiver. "I'm already frozen."

The plump manager was again standing in the open doorway. As they approached, he said, "I called, and they said a Homicide team would be along. I'm Bert Henshaw." He nodded toward the woman looking out the window. "My wife Gert."

Starsky nodded acknowledgment. Hutch said, "I'm Detective Hutchinson, and my partner is Detective Starsky. Anywhere we can squeeze a little of the water out of our clothes?"

"There's dryers in the laundry room," the manager

said. "Nobody be using them this time of night. I could loan you towels to wear while your clothes are drying." Turning to his wife, he said, "Get a couple of towels, Gert."

The woman moved into another room and returned carrying two large folded towels. She handed them to her husband, who still stood in the doorway, and he relayed them to Starsky and Hutch.

"What was going on out here?" the manager asked. "Did you fellows shoot that fellow in the pool?"

"No," Starsky said. "You can read about it in the papers. Mind showing us where the laundry room is?"

"Oh, sure." He stepped outdoors and headed for the east wing of the building.

Hutch said to Mrs. Henshaw, "When more cops show, will you tell them we're in the laundry room?"

"Sure," she said.

The laundry room was as large as the average public laundromat, with two dozen washing machines and six dryers. They were probably all busy in the daytime, since the complex must have housed at least a couple of hundred people, but it was now around midnight, and the room was deserted. Bert Henshaw pointed out an alcove where the detectives could undress without being seen.

Ten minutes later they were seated on wooden chairs, wrapped in towels, morosely watching their clothes tumble in a dryer through the machine's round window when two Homicide officers came into the laundry room. They were briefly told what had happened and left.

There was silence for a few moments after the Homicide officers had gone. Finally Starsky asked, "Your watch waterproof?"

"I don't know," Hutch said. "Before, I always took it off when I went swimming."

"Mine is, so I'm okay. But when you get home, bet-

107

ter take off the back and douse the works with mineral oil. Then take it into a jeweler tomorrow and get it cleaned."

"I don't have any mineral oil," Hutch said.

"Well, use cooking oil or salad oil."

"I don't cook with oil or put it on my lettuce."

Starsky gave him an exasperated look. "You plan to clean your gun when you get home?"

"Of course."

"Then you must have gun oil. Use it."

"Okay," Hutch said. "Incidentally, you're welcome."

Starsky looked at him, then formed a small smile. "Yeah, Hutch, thanks for saving my life again. Guess I still owe you two."

The apartment manager came in, went over to open the rotating dryer, and felt the clothes. He closed it again, and the machine resumed turning.

"Ought to be fairly dry in about ten minutes, Officer Hutchinson," the man said to Starsky.

Starsky said in an irritated tone, "I'm Starsky. He's Hutch."

"Oh, sorry. What do you think I ought to do about the pool, Officer Starsky? Think the filter can handle it all?"

"Handle what all?"

"Blood. All that blood's bound to throw the chemical balance off something fierce."

Starsky, who had begun to dislike the man, glowered at him. "I don't know anything about swimming pools."

"But you're a cop. I figured you'd know about blood."

Starsky's baleful look drove the man to the door. A trifle uncertainly he said, "Okay, I'll let you guys be now." He pointed toward the rear wall. "Phone back there if you want to call headquarters or something. Hooked through the switchboard, and there's nobody on that after ten P.M., so you'll have to dial 8 for an outside line. Okay?"

"Yeah, fine," Starsky said curtly.

As the manager left the room, Hutch's head slowly lifted, and the expression forming on his face suggested that a picture was coming into focus in his mind.

"Oh, no!" he said with a groan. "Damn!"

Giving him a surprised look, Starsky said, "What?"

"That's it! That's what Fat Rolly didn't do! He didn't dial enough numbers."

"When? What are you—"

Hutch interrupted with a rush of words. "When he got released and he made the phone call. He not only didn't dial 8 for an outside line, he didn't dial a full number. He should have dialed eight numbers if he was calling out, and he only dialed three."

"You sure?" Starsky asked. "How close were you to him?"

With the exasperation of one who has found an answer and resents not having it instantly accepted, Hutch said, "At the opposite end of the phone bank, but that makes no difference. I didn't see *what* numbers he dialed, but I know how many he dialed. And it was only three."

Starsky stared at him. "He's called us a few times, when he was in the mood to pass along tips. Maybe he knows some other cops."

"Nuts," Hutch said. "What he knows is who the killers are, and who it is that's setting us up. And it's somebody *inside* the department."

"Aw, come on, Hutch," Starsky said. "Why would anyone inside the department want us dead?"

"Who knows? But it's been staring us in the face all along. How did the shotgun twins know we'd be coming off that elevator in the basement of Tallman's apartment building? How'd they know we'd be on stakeout duty here tonight? They knew because we call in to headquarters, that's how they knew. And somebody is feeding them our whereabouts every time we call in!"

Starsky looked stunned, but he also looked convinced. He said slowly. "Captain Dobey or Henderson, that what you figure?"

"Either or both. Or the chief of detectives, or the chief of police, or the police commissioner. How the hell do I know? All I know is whoever tried to kill us has a pipeline."

After a long silence, Starsky asked quietly, "Who can we report to, then? Who in hell are we supposed to trust?"

"Same people we always trusted," Hutch said. "Us."

Chapter 15

IT WAS TWENTY minutes to one when Starsky and Hutch got back to the Torino. Starsky was about to radio in and have them logged out at that hour when Hutch hefted the plastic-wrapped shoe box and reminded him that they had to turn it in as evidence before going home. So instead they drove to Parker Center.

After reporting what they had to the Narcotics Division on the third floor, they delivered the package to the crime lab on the fourth. Then, as long as they were in the building, they decided to make their formal statements concerning the killing of Mooney and sign them, so they went back down to Homicide on third.

It was two-thirty in the morning when Starsky finally delivered Hutch to his cottage in Venice. As the Torino pulled in next to it, Starsky asked, "Vinnie's Gym about seven-thirty?"

Hutch shook his head. "I have a house guest, remember. No gym tomorrow. Pick me up here."

Starsky looked at the darkened cottage. "Sure you've got a house guest?"

"I told her not to bother waiting up. But hang on a minute and I'll let you know."

Hutch walked along the edge of the canal to the gate in the white picket fence and lifted the flowerpot just inside of it, where he had deposited the key when he left the house. Setting the pot down again, he smiled at Starsky and formed his right thumb and forefinger into an O.

Starsky blinked his lights in acknowledgment and drove off.

At seven-thirty the next morning Hutch stepped from the shower and began drying himself with a towel, still humming the lively tune he had hummed while showering. A light tap came at the bathroom door.

"Okay," he said.

The door opened and an attractive redhead wearing an airline stewardess's skirt, nothing but a bra on top, and no shoes, stepped into the bathroom. Hutch had one foot up on the seat of the commode, drying his thigh. She examined the process with interest for a moment, then said, "Hi."

"Hi, yourself," Hutch said, moving the towel down to dry his calf and foot.

"Thought you'd want to know your partner is here."

Nodding, he put his foot on the floor and raised the other one. He began humming the tune again. After watching him for a moment, she turned and walked back into the bedroom, humming the same tune he was.

A few minutes later Hutch entered the kitchen, wearing nothing but a pair of trousers. He found Starsky there, sitting at the breakfast counter, eating a wedge of cold pizza. A plastic cup, with a straw through the vent in the center of the lid, was on the counter in front of him.

"Where'd you get that?" Hutch asked, knowing it hadn't come from his refrigerator.

"Brought it from home. Cold pizza and root beer."

Hutch stared at him. "Now that's what I call a terrific breakfast, cold pizza and root beer."

He went over to the refrigerator, took out a blender pitcher filled with an off-white liquid, put it on the blender motor, and switched it on.

"It's the all-American breakfast," Starsky said. "Just for the autopsy record, what do you mash up in there every morning?"

"Oh, a little goat's milk, black strap molasses, sea kelp, lecithin, desiccated liver, and of course a good sprinkling of all your vitamins and trace elements."

Starsky made a face. "Of course."

Hutch drank the contents of his glass, unaffected by the sounds of gagging issuing from his partner's direction, then put it in the sink, and glanced at his watch. "We better get rolling. We're supposed to meet Huggy Bear in thirty minutes."

"How come you're wearing your watch?" Starsky asked. "Forget what I told you?"

Hutch shook his head. "Looked at the back and it said, 'Waterproof.' "

He started for the door.

The Internal Revenue Service, the state Alcoholic Beverages Control Board, and the Department of Motor Vehicles all knew Huggy Bear's real name, but no one else did, including his bank and his employees. He signed the paychecks "Huggy Bear." He was a tall, lean black man with close-cropped hair and elfin eyes. Usually he was a rather sporty dresser, given to loud checks and colorful bow ties, but this morning he wore only slacks, a T-shirt and a mournful expression.

He sat on a stool behind the bar, next to the telephone, but he wasn't working. Dianne was on duty as bartender. Huggy Bear was merely waiting.

The phone rang, and he answered it, "Chez Huggy Bear's."

Then his tone became respectful. "Sure, Mr. Tallman. I'll deliver the message. Expect 'em any minute."

He hung up, and the phone immediately rang again. Answering it, he said, "Chez Huggy Bear's—man, how the hell do I know?"

Laying the phone on the back bar, he said to Dianne, "Some broad called Sweetmeat here? Her old man's on the phone."

It wasn't quite eight-thirty, and at that hour of the morning only four customers were in the place. Two middle-aged but rather attractive black women sat together at the bar, and a middle-aged white couple was in one of the booths.

Looking at the two bar customers, Dianne asked, "Either of you Sweetmeat?"

"We both is, but that ain't either of our names," one of the women said, and giggled.

Dianne said to Huggy Bear, "I know the one in the booth. Named Hazel."

Lifting the phone again, Huggy Bear said, "Ain't here," and hung up.

The front door opened, letting a blinding shaft of sunlight into the dim interior of the café. Squeezing his eyes shut, Huggy Bear yelled, "Close that damn door!"

The door closed behind Starsky and Hutch, and the two detectives walked over to the bar.

Starsky said, "Is that any way to talk? You can't come through the damn door without opening it."

"You got something against daylight?" Hutch asked. "It happens every twenty-four hours."

"I got something against *today*," Huggy Bear said. "Spent two days at Catalina and never got out of the hotel room. Could just as easy rented a motel room down the block, and a tenth the cost. Pulled in at seven this morning, ready to lay down my head for at least twelve hours, and I find a message from my good buddies that I got to stay up to meet 'em. Then the phone keeps ringing like I'm an answering service. You are looking at a meeeean mistreater! So careful! Mean Joe Green is a pussycat compared to this Huggy Bear." He gave them a saintly grin, and his tone suddenly became sociable. "Anyways, wha's happening, boys?"

"See you in private?" Hutch asked.

"Sure," the black man said agreeably. "See if you can find an empty booth."

They glanced around. Every booth but one was empty.

"We'll try," Hutch said dryly.

He and Starsky walked over to the rearmost booth and sat together on the side facing the door, Starsky on the wall side. Huggy Bear came from behind the bar, followed along, and slid into the other side.

Chapter 16

HUGGY BEAR SAID, "One of those answering service messages I took was from Gerald Tallman, about a minute before you two come in. Wants you to phone him."

"Oh?" Hutch said. "Say what for?"

The black man shook his head. "He put it like a polite request, though. Not, 'Have them phone me,' but, 'Will you ask them to phone me, please?'"

"He's always been polite," Starsky said. "I hear that when he just started out in the rackets, as a two-bit strong-arm man, he always apologized after beating in some guy's head."

Hutch said, "What we came to see you about, Huggy, is somebody's trying to kill us."

"Yeah, I know," the black man said. "First thing I heard when I got back."

"You hadn't heard it before you went away?" Starsky asked.

Huggy Bear gave him a wounded look. Making an apologetic gesture, Starsky said, "Scratch that."

"I should think," Huggy Bear said. "Anyways, soon as I heard it, I made a couple of phone calls. Funny thing."

"What?" Hutch asked.

"Story's all over the street that there's a contract

on you. Even little guys like numbers runners and pimps know about it. Now a really big hit—and believe me, hitting two cops in this town is really big— maybe a couple of real high guys who weren't involved might know about it, because generally they clear with each other. But not runners and pimps, for catssake. Even *I* shouldn't have heard about it."

The two detectives thought this over. Presently Starsky asked, "What do you think?"

"The story was planted. On purpose."

"Why?" Hutch asked with a frown. "That doesn't make sense."

"Could make it," Huggy Bear disagreed. "Gerry Tallman's getting credit for the tries."

"Yeah, Tallman himself gave us that theory," Starsky said in a dissatisfied tone. "I can't buy it."

"Maybe you didn't think it through," Huggy Bear said. "The big guys in the rackets don't like their colleagues to make waves. And believe me, burning a couple of cops is gonna raise a surf. When a colleague gets too far out of line, the other big guys just may put out a contract on *him,* just to shut him up. What happened to Bugsy Siegel."

Starsky and Hutch looked at each other, then back at the lean black man. Hutch said slowly, "Somebody who couldn't get away with burning Tallman himself, but could move into his slot if others did it for him. Who's next in line?"

"Manny Torro," Huggy Bear said promptly.

Frowning, Starsky said, "Trouble with that theory is they wouldn't actually have to kill us, just convince everybody they meant to. And these guys are really trying. What hit team works with sawed-off double-barreled shotguns, Huggy?"

"Only one I ever heard about was Zale and Canelli, but if they was after you, they'd have gotten you."

Starsky and Hutch exchanged looks. Starsky said,

"That's what Tallman said, if he was talking about the same pair."

"Let's ask him when we phone him," Hutch said.

Starsky said to Huggy Bear, "Now we've got some kind of delicate questions to ask. About a couple of our superior officers."

"Who?"

"Captain Dobey, and Mark Henderson of the D.A.'s office."

"What about 'em?"

"Are either on the take?"

The black man gave Starsky a quizzical look. "There's lines, man. I don't talk about cops *to* cops."

Hutch said, "We think one of them is part of this, Huggy."

Huggy Bear's eyes grew wide. "You mean one of *them* put out the contract?"

"Maybe not that. But at least has been leaking where we are to the hit men."

After thinking this over, Huggy Bear said, "Makes a difference. That important, guess I can bend the rules."

"What about them?" Starsky asked.

Huggy Bear said carefully, "It's still a line I don't like to cross. Don't think I'd talk about it if I knew something real bad about them, because a bad cop hears you're badmouthin' him, he can really roust you. But I never heard much bad about those guys. Dobey's a pretty good cop. Family man, nuts about his wife and kids. He ain't on the take, or laying off, or anything like that."

"How about Assistant D.A. Henderson?" Hutch asked.

"He's got too much money to be on the take. And he's engaged to as much as he's got. The D.A. thing is like slumming, far as he's concerned. Mr. Henderson's eye is on higher office."

Looking at his partner, Hutch said, "That leaves us nowhere. Maybe we better phone Tallman to see what he wants."

He and Starsky got up from the booth.

Huggy Bear said, "You can use the bar phone."

"I think we want this private," Starsky said. "He leave a number?"

"Yeah, his unlisted one, but I already knew it. 826-9936."

Starsky and Hutch went over to the phone booth and crowded in together. Dropping a coin, Starsky dialed the number, then held the receiver so that Hutch could hear also.

A feminine voice answered, "Mr. Tallman's residence."

"Sounds like Maxine," Starsky said.

"It is. Who's this?"

"Starsky. Mr. Tallman left word to call."

"Oh, yes," the black maid said. "Just a moment."

There was a short wait, then Gerald Tallman's voice said, "Morning, Mr. Starsky. I think I have resolved the contract matter so that you won't have to worry about any more assassination attempts."

"Oh? How?"

"I'm not at liberty to disclose how, but I'm sure you can stop worrying."

"We need more than that, Mr. Tallman," Starsky said. "We're not about to relax until whoever gave out the contract is on ice."

"I can assure you he's quite cold."

Several seconds passed as Starsky thought that over. Then his eyes widened with a sudden idea. He looked at his partner, and saw by the expression on the blond man's face that he was having the same idea.

He said into the phone, "Wonder if you could put me in touch with one of your associates, Mr. Tallman? Manny Torro."

"Manny flew to South America this morning," Tallman said smoothly.

"Oh? What flight?"

"Private plane."

"I see," Starsky said. "When are you expecting him back?"

"I'm not. He's been put in charge of an operation down there."

"Well, could you give me an address where I could contact him?"

"Afraid not," Tallman said in a regretful tone. "It's a quite secret operation, and not exactly—legitimate. You understand, I'm sure."

"I think I do," Starsky said glumly.

Rather belatedly, Starsky thought, Tallman asked, "What did you want with Manny? Perhaps I could help you."

"I think not," Starsky said, and hung up.

When they left the booth, Hutch said, "He got the same idea as Huggy Bear."

"Yeah, and took instant action. Sort of wish he hadn't moved so fast."

"Why?" Hutch asked.

"Kind of rough on Manny, if it turns out that wasn't the answer."

After thinking this over, Hutch said, "Might be kind of rough on us, too. Would mean those two characters still plan to do some skeet shooting. You never asked him about them, incidentally."

"Didn't seem necessary after what he told us."

They had meandered over to the bar as they talked. When Dianne gave them an inquiring look, both shook their heads, indicating they wanted nothing to drink. Glancing around, they saw no sign of the proprietor.

"Where's Huggy Bear?" Starsky asked Dianne.

"Gone upstairs. Said if you fellows want anything else, write him a letter."

"Didn't know he could read," Hutch said, grinning. "Let's move, Starsk.

The two detectives started toward the door. But halfway there, Starsky stopped abruptly. Hutch examined the thoughtful expression on his partner's face with curiosity.

"What's the matter?" he asked.

"Just struck me I should have asked Tallman about those two shotgun artists."

"Why?"

"Because if the brainstorm I just had proves out, Manny Torro wasn't the answer, and he's cold for nothing."

He felt in his pocket, brought out a nickel, and asked, "You got a dime?"

Hutch felt in his pocket and produced another nickel. Handing it to Starsky, he said, "Two nickels will work."

Starsky headed back for the phone booth. Hutch followed behind him.

Over his shoulder Starsky said, "Tell you something, Hutch. When I was in high school, I played defensive back on the football team. We got to the last game of the year, and we were unbeaten, and the guys we were playing were unbeaten. They had this black kid playing end for them. Warrick, his name was, and he ran the hundred in 9.9. I couldn't keep up with him if I was riding a cannonball."

He stepped into the booth, leaving the door open. This time Hutch stayed outside, leaning against the edge of the booth. Starsky dropped in the two nickels and dialed.

With the phone to his ear, he said to Hutch, "So the thing was, I knew I couldn't be suckered in, see?" Then he said into the phone, "Starsky, Maxine. Let me talk to Mr. Tallman again."

He listened, then said, "Well, there's a phone in

122

that little room off the sauna, because I saw it. He can come out long enough to answer one question. Take about five seconds. Tell him it's urgent."

Turning back to Hutch, he said, "They kept sending this kid out in my area, and he'd go by me, and I'd run after him, and I'd start to listen, Hutch, because there's a sound the crowd makes when the ball's in the air, like ten thousand people get hit in the gut at the same time. And I'd know by that sound the ball was in the air, and I'd been suckered."

Returning his attention to the phone, he said into it, "Mr. Tallman, sorry to disturb you again, but one quick question. The guys you said couldn't miss us. Are their names Canelli and Zale?"

After a moment he said, "Thank you," and hung up.

Hutch straightened away from his leaning position on the edge of the booth as Starsky stepped out of it. Starsky said, "I just heard the sound, Hutch. We've been suckered."

"Instruct me," Hutch said.

"Everybody says those two don't miss. Yet they missed us three times. I say they don't miss unless they're *supposed* to."

Hutch looked at him without understanding. "Why were they supposed to?"

"Because Dobey or Henderson didn't want to kill you and me, but one or both of those two kids who *did* get splashed. And right now there's no one investigating those killings because they've got everybody thinking it was mistaken identity. There's two cold slabs of meat in the coroner's cooler that nobody gives a damn about."

Understanding hit Hutch. In a wondering voice he said, "They weren't after you?"

"Never."

They looked at each other, both adjusting to this

entirely new train of thought, mentally checking it for holes.

"Does it hold?" Starsky finally asked.

Hutch nodded. "I'm afraid it does."

"Where do you want to start?"

"Those two kids," Hutch said. "The coroner's cooler."

Starsky nodded. They headed for the door together.

Chapter 17

As Starsky pulled onto the Hall of Justice parking lot, he said, "You know police headquarters used to be here, along with the courtrooms, and the morgue, and all the other stuff still here, before they built Parker Center?"

"Yeah, I know," Hutch said. "Must have been crowded."

Starsky managed to find a parking place. They walked over to a side entrance and took the stairway to the basement. Spotting a drinking fountain, Starsky stopped, bent over it, and pressed the foot lever. It was one of those refrigerated fountains shaped like a large box standing on end. No water came out of the drinking spout, but Starsky felt it gush over his shoes.

Backing away, Starsky looked at the puddle on the floor. Hutch, not seeing what had happened and thinking Starsky had wanted only a sip, bent over the fountain.

Stepping back an instant later, he looked at the now wider puddle on the floor, then glared at Starsky. "Thanks for the warning, buddy," he said.

Starsky grinned innocently. "I thought you wanted your feet washed."

A man in coveralls came along at that moment

and pasted a sticker on the front of the fountain reading OUT OF ORDER.

"Perfect timing," Starsky said. "I told you this morning I had a hunch it was going to be one of those days."

They moved on to the morgue, identified themselves, and were allowed into the storage room. The attendant in charge was a wizened little man in his early sixties who resembled a gnome.

After showing their ID's, Starsky said, "Couple of kids came in night before last. Killed by shotgun blasts while parked in a red and white Torino on a beach north of Santa Monica." He turned to Hutch. "I don't even know those kids' names. Shows how much attention any cops paid to them."

"Stanley Cather and Patricia Talbot," the attendant said. "Names are fresh in my mind because they just came back."

"Back?" Hutch said, staring at him. "From where?"

"The P.M. Post mortem." He looked down at their shoes. "Is it raining outside? Both of you got wet shoes."

"No, it's not raining," Hutch said.

"Ought to be careful, walking around with wet shoes. Catch your death of cold. Which you want to see first?"

"The boy, I guess," Starsky said in a reluctant tone suggesting he'd really prefer to see neither.

Going over to a chart on the wall consisting of brass-edged slots into which removable cards were shoved, the attendant studied it. "Fifteen and sixteen," he said.

One entire wall contained metal drawers whose fronts were about two feet square. Going over to the one numbered 15, the little man slid it out.

Without much enthusiasm Starsky and Hutch looked

into the drawer. The naked body of a young man was in it, unrecognizable from the chest up.

After quick glances, both detectives looked away. "How'd they identify him?" Hutch asked.

"Fingerprints. He had a record."

Starsky gestured for the attendant to slide the drawer back in. The man did, and slid out the one next to it. It contained the nude body of a young woman with a strawberry birthmark just below her navel. The upper part of her body was as mutilated as the young man's.

The attendant said, "Trim little figure she had. Wonder what her face looked like."

Starsky gestured for him to close the drawer. He asked, "Identification verified through fingerprints, too?"

Sliding the drawer closed, the little man shook his head. "Driver's license in her purse told who she was. Positive identification made by her roommate. By that birthmark on her tummy you may have noticed." He bent to peer at the label on the front of drawer 16. "Nineteen years old. Female Caucasian. Used to call 'em white."

Hutch asked, "P.M. turn anything?"

The little man peered up at him. With a touch of sarcasm he said, "She was killed by a shotgun blast at close range."

Hutch was examining him glumly, seemingly on the verge of telling him to shove it, when the attendant added casually, "She was about two months' pregnant. No wedding ring or engagement ring, either."

Neither had any comment to make to that. Starsky asked, "Can we see the girl's personal effects?"

"Don't think so. Her roommate was out there at the front desk picking them up when you two came in. Probably gone by now."

After a quick glance at one another, Starsky and

Hutch raced for the door. The attendant called after them, "Careful! That tile's slippery if you got wet shoes!"

As they burst out of the storage room, they spotted a short, dumpy girl of about twenty at the far end of the corridor, heading for the exit. In her arms she carried a large paper bag. She turned when she heard pounding footsteps behind her, and backed against the wall with a frightened look in her eyes.

Hutch unnecessarily called, "Hold it, please, miss!"

When the two detectives came to a halt, rather hemming her in, she looked at them from wide, apprehensive eyes. Both detectives showed their ID's.

"Police officers, miss," Starsky said. "Are you Patricia Talbot's roommate?"

The girl looked a little less frightened, but still wary. "Yes."

Nodding toward the paper bag she was clutching, Hutch asked, "Are those her personal effects?"

"Yes," the girl admitted.

Starsky said, "We'd like to take a look at them, please."

"Well, I'm not sure," the girl said uncertainly. "I mean, I signed a receipt for them back there."

Starsky asked, "What's your name, miss?"

"Knebel. Gretchen Knebel."

"Well, Miss Knebel, we never knew Patricia Talbot, but we know she was murdered, and we'd like to find out who did it. I think that makes us her friends, too."

"A lot of cops say things like that," Gretchen said warily.

Starsky said, "A lot of cops say, 'Oh, what a beautiful morning,' too, but you ought to be able to tell the difference between the ones who really know the melody, and the ones who are just saying the words. Besides, we don't want to keep the stuff. We just want to look at it."

Relenting, Gretchen said, "Well, all right. But how come the police didn't hang onto Patty's stuff?"

Hutch's and Starsky's eyes met. "Interesting point," Hutch said thoughtfully. "Why *didn't* the department order them held?"

They both knew the answer. Someone with official clout had to authorize their release.

But before either had a chance to comment, the dumpy girl said, "Look, the reason I wanted all this junk was so that I could go through it before her folks did."

"Why?" Hutch asked.

"Because you know parents. Suppose they found a joint in her purse? Or suppose they found she was taking the pill? They're going to have it bad enough without anything like that."

Starsky lifted the paper bag from the girl's unresisting arms, set it on a bench next to the wall, and took a purse out of it. He began taking items from it and laying them on the bench.

Hutch said dryly, "If she was taking a pill, it was aspirin. She was pregnant."

"Patty was?" Gretchen said in a surprised voice. Then, after a reflective pause, "She was always kind of careless."

His attention on the items Starsky was taking from the purse, Hutch asked, "Any idea who the father could be?"

The dumpy girl shrugged. "Some guy. Over fourteen, under fifty. I'd narrow it down that much, I guess."

Starsky finished emptying the purse, set it down, and poked in the bag again. The only thing else in it was the clothing the girl had been wearing, most of it stiff with dried blood. After briefly examining it, he shoved it back into the bag.

"I got a notion," Hutch said to his partner.

Glancing around at him, Starsky said, "Tell me."

"We've just been assuming the department ran makes on both kids, because the morgue attendant mentioned that Cather was identified by fingerprints. Maybe they didn't."

"On my way," Starsky said, immediately heading for the desk, where there was a phone.

"Check out Zale and Canelli, too," Hutch called after him.

"*Sí.*"

The girl on duty at the desk looked up from the magazine she was reading as Starsky stopped in front of her and lifted the phone on the desk.

"Dial 8 for an outside line," she said.

Starsky gave her a pained smile. He dialed 8, then the number of Parker Center.

Meantime Hutch was examining the items from the dead girl's purse that Starsky had laid out on the bench. There were the usual things: a wallet with a few dollars in it, a driver's license and various cards, a comb, a small mirror, a lace handkerchief, keys, a lipstick, and a miscellaneous assortment of other items, including a number of papers.

As he started going through the papers, Hutch asked, "You close friends with Miss Talbot?"

"Not really," Gretchen said. "They just assigned us. We didn't take the same courses or anything. I'm a phys ed major. She was taking pre-law."

At the other end of the hallway Starsky was saying into the phone, "A priority one make on the following individuals: Patricia Talbot, deceased."

Hutch slipped a personal letter he had just read back into its envelope and laid it aside. He started thumbing through a small notebook which seemed to contain lecture notes.

"You said pre-*law*, is that correct?" he asked Gretchen.

The girl nodded. "Not that she was a big book drudge, though. Because lawyers are rich and she always wanted a rich husband."

"She said that?" he inquired.

"Often."

At the other end of the hall Starsky was continuing on the phone: "And Zale. Z as in Zebra, A as in Adam, L as in Lincoln, E as in Edgar. Should have a long run on both him and Canelli. Probably be in the red file."

Hutch was still studying the notebook. "They ever have guest instructors out at the university?" he asked.

"Hardly ever in phys ed."

"How about pre-law?"

"I don't know," Gretchen said. "I take phys ed."

Hutch set down the notebook and opened a folded sheet of paper. The sheet was divided into four columns. In the first column were listed class subjects. The second listed the days and times the classes met. The third showed buildings and room numbers. The fourth listed the instructors.

"What's this here?" Hutch said, really meaning it as an exclamation rather than as a question, since he already knew the answer.

Peering at it, Gretchen said, "Looks like a class schedule."

Hutch ran his finger down the list of subjects until he came to *Princioles of Western Law*. In the next column was listed *Mon., Wed., Fri.—10 a.m.* In the third column was *Adams Hall, Rm. 5*. The last column listed the instructor as *Mark Henderson*. The "o" in Henderson had been doodled in the shape of a heart.

Starsky came running along the hall toward them. "It's Henderson!" he called in a jubilant voice when he was only halfway to them.

Chapter 18

HUTCH AND GRETCHEN both turned in surprise to look at Starsky bearing down on them at a near gallop.

When Starsky came to a panting halt, Hutch said, "Yeah, it's Henderson, but how did you know?"

Starsky took a moment to recover his breath before saying, "Well, I don't know how he got to the girl—"

"I do," Hutch interrupted. "He teaches a class she was in at the university."

Starsky looked interested. "Okay, that answers that. Love happens. She blooms. Won't go away, won't get rid of the kid. He's got a marriage coming up. The girl's got to go."

"Fill me in," Hutch said.

"Zale and Canelli. He had them up on murder two. Tight rap. Charges were dropped on the recommendation of Assistant District Attorney Henderson."

Hutch asked, "What about the driver, the kid who stole the Torino?"

"He was on probation for dealing pot when he got busted on two counts of grand theft, auto. Should have drawn at least two years, but he was on probation at the request of Assistant District Attorney Henderson."

Hutch, now speaking with rapid enthusiasm, said, "He has the kid steal a car identical to yours. Has him take the girl out to the beach, where he's got Canelli and Zale waiting." Suddenly his enthusiasm abated a little and he frowned. "How'd he talk the kid into suicide?"

Starsky made an impatient gesture. "Gave him some kind of snow job. Doesn't matter how he sold him, but you can bank on it the kid wasn't expecting a shotgun blast. Canelli and Zale blow the two kids apart, and Henderson gets everyone in the department thinking I was the intended victim and you were next in line so that we couldn't testify at the Tallman trial."

They looked at each other for a long time, mentally replaying the mixture of evidence and assumptions one more time. Finally Hutch said in a tone of satisfaction. "I think it holds."

With a touch of excitement Starsky said, "I heard that sound, Hutch. The ball's in the air."

Together they headed for the door, taking long strides. Gretchen Knebel, who all during the rapid-fire conversation had been swiveling her head back and forth like a spectator at a tennis match, gazed after them until they disappeared through the door. Then she began to pick the items up off the bench and return them to the purse.

As they climbed into the Torino outside in the parking lot, Starsky said, "You having the same thought I am about our next move?"

"If you're thinking about Fat Rolly," Hutch said.

"I am," Starsky said grimly. He backed up, swung toward the parking lot exit and drove off the lot. "Rolly has to be the one who spread the phony story about there being a contract on us. Probably Henderson used him as a go-between for Canelli and Zale, too. He probably wouldn't risk being seen with them himself."

"Think we can get the tub of lard to talk?" Hutch asked.

"If we can't, we'll render him down to soap."

Fat Rolly's Bargain Circus was in a large, ram-shackle one-story building in the center of the district. In the front part of the building was a secondhand store offering every type of used goods imaginable, from furniture to clothing. Behind it was a second store which the general public never saw. To get in you either had to be a preferred customer or bring an introduction from someone whose judgment Rolly trusted. The items in the rear store were also used, but they were as a rule newer, in top condition, and hot.

Starsky drove the Torino up the alley behind the Bargain Circus and onto the hard-packed dirt area behind the building. He parked next to a truck loading platform. The two detectives got out of the car and climbed the wooden steps at one end of the platform.

There was a sliding door through which larger pieces of merchandise could be passed in and out, closed and padlocked at the moment. Beyond it was an ordinary doorway with both a door and a screen door. As it was now midmorning, the sun was well up, and it was starting to get quite warm, but the screen door barred the way inside.

That is, the screen door was the only inanimate bar. There was also a large, bulky man with a pushed-in face, seated on a folding bridge chair, reading a comic book. The chair was tilted backward against the latch-side edge of the door, so that entry into the building was impossible unless he moved.

The man looked up from his comic book when the Torino pulled in and parked. His gaze fixed on the two detectives as they got out of the car, followed them as they climbed the steps and approached him, then deliberately returned to the comic book when they came to a halt before him.

"Hiya, Marty?" Hutch said genially. "Open sesame and announce us to the merchant prince."

135

Without looking up, Marty said, "Get lost. Go on. Beat it, or I'll rip your chest off."

Hutch and Starsky exchanged looks. "How do you rip a chest off?" Starsky asked his partner curiously.

Shrugging, Hutch snaked out a toe, hooked it around one of the upraised front legs of the tilted chair, and jerked the chair out from under the bulky man. The chair skidded off the edge of the loading platform and tumbled to the ground below, and the comic book went flying. Marty landed with a thump on his buttocks.

"That's to get your attention," Hutch said.

Springing to his feet with rather remarkable agility for such a large man, Marty whipped out a leather sap and swung it at Hutch. The blond man pulled back his head like a tortoise withdrawing into his shell, and the sap whistled harmlessly past his chin.

Hutch circled to place his back to the screen door as Marty bore in with the sap again raised. Starsky fingered the butt of his .38, but decided to let Hutch handle it.

As Marty swung the sap for a second time, Hutch ducked beneath it, slipped to one side, and grabbed the man's shirtfront with his left hand. He jerked him into a bent-over position, placed his right palm against his butt, and shoved. As Marty dived headfirst into the screen door, Hutch increased his momentum by giving him a tremendous kick in the rump.

Marty went inside, right through the screen door, leaving a large gap in it.

"That's to open the door," Hutch said.

The hole in the door was large enough for the detectives to pass through, too, but only if they ducked down low. Hutch pulled it open to go in, and Starsky followed behind him.

Another large man, this one with a bulbous nose and elephant ears, was standing flat against the wall to the right of the door. As Hutch went by, he raised a baseball bat.

He kept it raised, frozen in position, when Starsky whipped out his gun and flicked off the safety. "Bad, Leo," Starsky said chidingly. "That's bad."

His gaze fixed on the gun, Leo slowly lowered the bat to his side and let it drop to the floor. Turning his back to Starsky, he put both hands behind him, familiar with the drill from long practice. Starsky pushed the safety back on, put the gun away, and snapped on cuffs.

As Marty climbed dazedly to his feet, Hutch picked up the dropped leather sap, walked over to within two feet of the bulky man, and began contemplatively slapping the sap lightly into his left palm. After gazing sourly at the rhythmic movement for a few seconds, Marty also turned his back and put his hands behind him. Tossing aside the sap, Hutch handcuffed him.

Both detectives then shook down their prisoners, but found no weapons other than the sap and baseball bat.

All this time Fat Rolly remained seated behind an old desk to one side of the room, his hands folded across his substantial belly and his expression resembling that of a disapproving schoolteacher watching horseplay among students. Today he wore a blue bandanna around his forehead, and his T-shirt bore the legend *Stud Service—By Appointment Only*.

Behind the desk, on both sides of it, and all around the walls were piled washing machines, dryers, TV sets, stereo outfits, bicycles, and assorted other items.

In a scathing tone the fence said, "Marty, I like you because you're so fast on your feet. You too, Leo. You're an ace."

Neither man said anything, merely gazed at the fat man sullenly.

There was a coffee machine against the wall directly

opposite the desk. Going over to it, Starsky dropped in a dime. Over his shoulder he said, "What's happening, Rolly?"

Rolly, a trifle pale, but trying to play it with nonchalance, leaned back in his swivel chair, swung his feet up on the desk, and crossed his ankles. "Business ain't too good," he said. "But like it says in the papers, the Gross National Product should be up by year's end."

Hutch said, "You would know about anything gross, Rolly."

Starsky was staring at the coffee machine in outrage. It had failed to drop a cup, and the coffee was squirting out into nothing and running down the drain.

Turning toward his partner, he said, "You see that!"

The blond man said with sympathy, "In a machine world, you have no mechanical touch, Starsk."

Hutch seated himself on a corner of the desk. In a conversational tone he said, "Did you know Manny Torro got scratched because of that story you spread around, Rolly? Gerry Tallman added two and two and got five. Poor Manny. And he hadn't done a damn thing."

"I didn't hear nothing about that," Rolly said warily. "What story?"

"The one about there being a contract out on Starsky and me. You spread it too wide, Rolly. Tallman realized that if there really was a contract out on two cops, every two-bit punk on the street wouldn't know about it. So he rightly figured it was a planted story. Only he guessed wrong about who planted it. Since it was obvious to him he was being set up, he figured the only logical framer had to be the guy next in line to him. So good-bye, Manny."

"That's too bad," the fat man said. "It's the risk those big-shot hoods take, though. Step out of line once, and it's curtains. I didn't spread that story. I just heard it, like everybody else."

Starsky, still over by the coffee machine, said, "Little shots like you take risks, too, Rolly, when you get involved with people like Zale and Canelli."

Fat Rolly gave him a sharp look. "Never heard of them."

Hutch said, "And run errands for a guy like Assistant District Attorney Mark Henderson."

Rolly looked up at him with no change of expression, but a bead of perspiration suddenly ran down his cheek. "Never heard of him either."

Spinning around, Hutch kicked the fat man's feet off the desk, then swung to his own feet. Rolly's feet hit the floor with a jolt. He straightened in his chair and stared at the blond detective with a mixture of trepidation and indignation.

"Don't get physical," he said.

"Yeah," the bulbous-nosed Leo said. "You guys got no right to push citizens around. That's police brutality."

Starsky walked over to Leo and gazed up into the taller man's face. The man looked abashed, as though he wished he had kept his mouth shut. Starsky walked behind him, removed his cuffs, and put them away.

"Take a walk," he said. "Far."

The man gave him an uncertain look, glanced at Fat Rolly, back at Starsky again, and decided he had better obey. He left rather hurriedly.

Hutch went over to Marty and uncuffed him. "You walk with him. Just as far."

Marty didn't even look at his employer. He just hurried after Leo.

"Why'd you do that?" Fat Rolly asked uneasily.

"Because we didn't want any witnesses," Starsky told him.

Chapter 19

GETTING UP FROM HIS CHAIR, Fat Rolly sidled toward the curtained doorway leading into the legitimate secondhand store occupying the front of the building. Hutch took three long strides to block the way, and Starsky bore in on the fat man from the other side. Without touching him, merely moving toward him inexorably, the two detectives backed Rolly into a corner.

"You better not hit me," Rolly said desperately, sweat now running down both cheeks. "There's laws against that."

"We're not going to hit you, Rolly," Starsky said, giving him a malevolent smile. "Why do you think we're going to hit you?"

Rolly's gaze jumped from one to the other. "You're going to do something," he said fearfully. "Why you looking at me like that?"

"Yeah, we're going to do something to you," Hutch agreed. "But it isn't going to be physical. We're going to put you away in the joint for the rest of your goddamned life."

"For what?" Rolly squealed. "I ain't done nothing."

"For accessory to murder one, Rolly," Starsky told him. "We've got you nailed to the wall."

Jerking the blue bandanna from around his fore-

head in order to mop his drenched face, Rolly said on
a high note, "I got nothing to do with no murder.
Whose murder?"

"Those two kids who were shotgun-blasted on the
beach night before last," Hutch said. "Stanley Cather
and Patricia Talbot. Twenty-two years old and nineteen years old, Rolly. Hardly even started out in life.
Both good-looking kids, too. The jury's not gonna be
happy with you, Rolly. There'll be no recommendation for leniency. You're going to get the book."

"I had nothing to do with that," the fat man said,
terrified. "You guys know I had nothing to do with
that."

"We can prove you were Henderson's go-between
when he sicked Zale and Canelli on us," Starsky shot
at him. "You think the jury's going to believe you
weren't the go-between for the first job, too?"

"I had no part of that," Rolly protested, frenziedly
mopping his face again. "I didn't even know about it.
I mean, I heard it on the air next morning, and read
about it in the newspaper, but I never knew it was
going to happen. I never even heard of those kids
until I turned on the radio next morning. You guys
know I wouldn't get involved in no murder. The other
thing was different. There was a guarantee nobody
would really get—"

He came to a terrified halt, appalled at his slip.
His eyes darted from Starsky to Hutch and back again,
hoping without real hope that they hadn't caught it.
Their uncompromising gazes bored into him.

Licking his lips, he whispered, "Deal?"

The forbidding looks on the two detectives' faces
instantly dissolved into bright, friendly smiles.

"Sure, Rolly," Starsky said wholeheartedly. "We
don't really want to see you rot your life away in the
joint. Just mean some other fence would open up in
our district, and we'd have to break him in on what

he could get away with, and what he'd get stepped on for. We kind of like the status quo. So we're going to get you off the hook entirely. We're not even going to bust you for all the hot merchandise in this place."

This sudden affability frightened Rolly nearly as much as their previous forbidding manner. "What do I have to do?" he asked warily.

Hutch said, "Just set up Henderson and the shotgun twins for us."

"Oh, my God!" Rolly said in abject terror. "Zale and Canelli would kill me!"

Starsky gave his head a slow shake. "Not where they're going, Rolly. If the jury would give you maximum for setting up those kids, how you suppose they're going to feel about the guys who actually pulled the triggers?"

Licking his lips again, Rolly's eyes moved back and forth from one to the other.

Hutch said, "Course if you'd rather go into the joint with Zale and Canelli, that's all right, too. But don't count on your clamming up saving you from their revenge. Starsky and I are just mean enough to leak word into the prison grapevine that you snitched on them."

Rolly's eyes grew enormous.

Starsky said, "He's not going to cooperate, Hutch. Let's cut the gaff, take him in, and book him for accessory to murder one."

Grabbing the fat man's shoulder, Starsky spun him around, jerked his arms behind his back, and clamped on the cuffs.

"I am too going to cooperate," Rolly squealed.

Taking his shoulder, Hutch spun him around to face them again. "I think you understand the charge, Rolly," he said. "You have the constitutional right to remain silent. If you do make a statement, it may be taken down and used against you in evidence. You are entitled to legal counsel at all stages of your arrest, arraignment, and trial procedure——." At that point Hutch departed slightly from the standard warning to add, "——from the time we reach the booking desk in the Felony Section until they throw you in the slammer for life." He concluded by reverting to the formula. "If you are unable to afford a lawyer, one will be furnished you at public expense."

"I said I'd cooperate," Rolly said plaintively. "Why are you guys doing this?"

As though they hadn't heard him, Starsky and Hutch each took one arm and marched him out the back door. They pushed him down the wooden steps and into the back seat of the Torino. Hutch got into the back seat with him, while Starsky slid under the steering wheel.

"Listen," Rolly said. "Will you guys listen to me?"

Starsky said, "Hutch told you that you have the constitutional right to remain silent, so shut up."

"But I want to talk," Rolly insisted. "I waive my right to remain silent. You're allowed to do that."

Hutch said, "You're too late, Rolly. You had your chance. We also have the constitutional right not to listen. So do like Starsky told you, and shut up."

The fat man lapsed into miserable silence. They drove to Parker Center without further conversation.

As they pulled onto the lot, a shiny avocado-green Jaguar sports car nosed up out of the underground garage. Starsky said, "Jiggers! There's Henderson!"

Hutch gripped the handcuffed man by the nape of the neck and hurled him face down on the floor of the back seat. As the Jaguar headed for the parking lot exit, one lane over, Henderson glanced over, spotted the Torino, smiled, and waved. Starsky and Hutch smiled and waved back.

Hutch lifted his foot from the middle of Rolly's back as they drove down the ramp into the garage.

Pulling the fat man upright, he shoved him back into the seat. Rolly gaped at him without understanding.

Parking next to the dispatcher's cubicle and leaving the engine running, Starsky climbed from the car as Hutch hauled the prisoner from the back seat. "Suspect for booking," Starsky said. "Park it where we can get at it fast, because we may have to leave in a hurry."

"Sure," the dispatcher said. "There's an empty slot right by the exit ramp."

They hustled the prisoner over to the elevator. En route Starsky glanced at his watch. "Only a quarter to twelve. Henderson breaks for lunch early."

"Maybe he'll come back early, then," Hutch said hopefully.

"Dreamer," Starsky said.

When they got on the elevator, Starsky punched the button for the third floor. Fat Rolly said, "Felony Section's on first."

"We're going to feed you lunch before we book you," Hutch informed him. "We have to eat, too, and we want your scintillating companionship."

"Cafeteria's on eight," Rolly said suspiciously.

"Our squad room's on three," Starsky explained. "We wash our hands before we go to lunch. You're going to wash both your hands and your face. You look like hell."

When they reached the squad room, Captain Dobey stuck his head out of his office door just as Starsky was unlocking Fat Rolly's cuffs. He examined the inscription on the suspect's T-shirt curiously.

"What you got?" he asked.

"Just a luncheon guest, Captain," Starsky said. "We'll explain later."

The captain said, "Cafeteria food's not all that bad that you have to drag guests in handcuffed."

"This is a special guest," Starsky told him. "After lunch he's going in the slammer."

Captain Dobey gave the prisoner another quizzical look, shrugged, and went back into his office.

Lifting a phone from one of the long tables in the squad room, Starsky dialed three numbers. After two rings a feminine voice said, "Traffic Bureau, Ruskin speaking."

"Starsky, Anne," Starsky said. "Do me a favor?"

"Sure, love. Virtually anything."

"Mark Henderson's office is right across the hall from you. He's out to lunch. Will you sort of keep watch and ring me at the squad room when he logs back in?"

"If it's before one, love. That's when I go to lunch myself."

"He ought to be back by then, sweets. Thanks."

Hanging up, he said to Fat Rolly, "Okay, lard, we'll show you the washroom, so you can make yourself presentable."

They were back down from the eighth-floor cafeteria by twelve-thirty. The three of them sat at one of the long tables, Starsky and Hutch idly conversing and ignoring Fat Rolly, until a phone call came for Starsky from the girl in the Traffic Bureau shortly after one o'clock.

"Henderson just walked into his office," she said. "I skipped five minutes of my lunch hour waiting for him, just as a special favor to you. Any reward?"

"You win my body," Starsky told her. "You can collect tonight." Then he remembered he had a date with Cindy. "No, tomorrow night. I forgot."

"Forgot what?"

"Night duty."

"Night duty, rats, you rat," she said. "You've got another date. Phone me in the morning and I'll let you know if I'm available tomorrow night."

She hung up.

Starsky stood up. "Okay, Rolly, let's get it over with."

The two officers led him from the squad room to the elevator, not bothering to handcuff him again. When they got on, Hutch punched the first-floor button.

"You guys really going through with this?" Rolly asked. "Even after I said I'd cooperate?"

Neither detective gave him any answer.

Downstairs at the jail, instead of leading the suspect directly to the Felony Section, they steered him over to the bank of phones on the shelf against the wall. Stopping in front of a free one, the eyes of both detectives bored into Rolly's.

"One last chance, Rolly," Hutch said.

"Sure," Rolly said eagerly. "I been telling you all along I'll cooperate."

Hutch said, "Phone Henderson. Tell him Zale and Canelli want to see him right now. They're threatening to blow the whistle if he isn't there within the next hour."

Fat Rolly licked his lips. "What if he asks questions?"

"All you know is what you told him. Zale and Canelli didn't give you any explanation, and you're too afraid of them to ask what it was about. He'll buy that."

Rolly nodded. "It's the living truth. What if he asks why I'm phoning from the jail?"

"You don't tell him you're phoning from the jail, asshole," Starsky said. "If he asks, you're phoning from your place."

Nodding, Fat Rolly picked up the phone and dialed three numbers. Starsky and Hutch bent their heads on either side of him to listen.

Henderson's voice answered on the other end, "District Attorney's Liaison Office. Henderson."

Fat Rolly relayed the message he had been instructed to give.

When he finished, Henderson said in a shaky voice, "What's the matter with them? What do they want?"

"All they told me was that, sir," Rolly said. "You'll have to find out from them."

"All right," Henderson said tightly. "Where are you calling from?"

"The Bargain Circus."

"Okay. Thanks for calling." Henderson hung up.

Fat Rolly hung up, too. Starsky and Hutch hustled him over to the Misdemeanor desk.

Hutch said to the booking sergeant, "Stick this suspect in the can on suspicion of possession of stolen property. We'll make out the papers later, because we haven't time now."

"You guys said I'd be off the hook," the fat man protested. "I cooperated."

"Beautifully," Starsky agreed. "But if you think you're going to be running around loose to make phone calls before we wrap this up, you must be nuts." He turned to the booking sergeant. "No phone calls. He just had his one call."

He and Hutch hurried to the elevator to take it down to the garage.

Chapter 20

STARSKY AND HUTCH moved quickly from the elevator to the vehicle dispatcher's cubicle in the garage. The dispatcher who had been on duty when they pulled in must have been on his lunch break, because a different man was in the cubicle.

Showing his ID, Starsky said, "Cruiser Three, a red and white Torino, and where is it?" He held out his hand. "Keys?"

"I'll have somebody bring it around," the dispatcher said.

"Give me the goddamned keys!" Starsky snapped at him. "And tell me where it's parked."

Startled, the man lifted a set of keys from a hook on a numbered board and handed them over. "You don't have to yell," he said in a petulant voice. "Slot twenty-eight, right by the exit ramp."

Starsky and Hutch double-timed in that direction. The Torino was parked alongside a thick concrete support post which was a good three feet in diameter. Hutch slipped behind the post. Starsky started the engine, then lay flat on the front seat. About three minutes passed.

Then Starsky heard the sound of a powerful car swishing by. Hutch jerked open the right-hand door. Sitting up, Starsky had the car in reverse by the time

Hutch had slid inside and slammed the door. The Torino backed up, swung toward the exit, and roared up the ramp in pursuit.

The avocado-green Jaguar headed south on Los Angeles Street. The Torino fell in behind. There was considerable traffic, as there always was in downtown Los Angeles, and Starsky kept three vehicles between the Torino and the car they were tailing.

Hutch said, "We ought to have my car instead of this circus wagon. He catches this one in the rearview mirror and we've had it."

"Want me to let you out, you can catch a bus to Venice and pick up your heap?" Starsky asked sarcastically.

"Funny, funny. Just stay far enough back so he can't make you out."

"Yes, sir," Starsky said, lifting his right hand from the wheel long enough to salute. "I never tailed a car before, sir, but under your expert leadership, I'm sure I can manage."

"Shut up and drive," Hutch said amiably.

Starsky said, "With him being a lawyer, what if he doesn't say anything incriminating while he's with Zale and Canelli?"

Hutch craned to see if the Jaguar was still the fourth car ahead.

Starsky said, "I mean, we could end up in the toilet if this doesn't work."

"It will." Hutch said. "It will."

Also peering ahead, Starsky said. "Cripes! The light at Fifth just turned yellow, and Henderson's already through it."

The three cars behind the Jaguar managed to scoot through the yellow light before it changed to red. It turned just as the Torino got to the intersection. Starsky had to slam on the brakes—the traffic on Fifth Street instantly began to roll across the intersection.

It was all from left to right, because at this point Fifth was a one-way street.

"Go through it!" Hutch said. "Use the siren!"

"If I use the siren, he'll know he's being tailed," Starsky objected. "Get the glasses out."

Bending to slide out the rack below the front seat, Hutch grabbed up a set of binoculars and put them to his eyes. "He's passed Sixth Street, still going straight."

Glaring up at the signal light, Starsky said, "Come on! Haven't you got another color?"

Hutch said, "He just turned right on Seventh! We're going to lose him if you don't hit that siren button!"

"He can't see us from there," Starsky said. "Maybe he'll think we're a fire engine."

He touched the siren button just enough to make the siren emit a low growl, and eased out past the crosswalk. Traffic continued to flow past. Starsky gave a good blast with the siren, and traffic stopped. He zoomed through the red light.

Starsky floored the accelerator for two blocks. At Seventh, which was two-way, the light was just turning red. He spun to the right through it, causing a taxi driver who started to shoot across the intersection the instant his light turned green to squeal his brakes and curse at him.

They sped along Seventh for several blocks, Starsky zooming in and out of traffic at fifty miles an hour, Hutch peering through the binoculars.

Finally lowering the glasses, Hutch said, "He'd be in sight by now if he'd stayed on Seventh. We've lost him."

Slowing, Starsky said wryly, "Sorry about that."

Hutch said, "Maybe he cut over to Wilshire. It doesn't come through all the way to Los Angeles Street, and he couldn't turn right on Sixth to get to the point where it ends, because Sixth is one-way in the other direction. He would have taken Seventh to Figueroa or beyond, turned right, then turned left again on Wilshire."

"What have we got to lose?" Starsky said.

They were approaching MacArthur Park. Starsky swung right at Alvarado Street to skirt the eastern edge of the park, and braked to a halt at the stop sign at Wilshire Boulevard.

The Jaguar crossed the intersection right in front of them, Mark Henderson looking straight ahead with a grim expression on his face.

"Bingo!" Starsky said. "We hit the jackpot!"

"That's a mixed metaphor," Hutch instructed him. "See if you can hang onto him this time."

Saluting again, Starsky said, "Yes, sir."

It was several seconds before Starsky was able to break through cross-traffic and turn left. When he finally managed to, the Jaguar was a good block and a half ahead. Starsky sent the speedometer needle to fifty again. Hutch lifted the binoculars to his eyes.

In his rearview mirror Starsky caught a glimpse of a flashing red light immediately behind them. In a tone of disbelief he said, "I don't barking believe it!"

Lowering the glasses, Hutch glanced at his partner, saw his gaze fixed on the rearview mirror, and swiveled in his seat to look out the back window. His face registered consternation at sight of the black and white police vehicle.

"If you don't pull over, they'll hit the siren and scare the hell out of Henderson," he said tightly. "Better stop."

Starsky cramped the wheel to pull over into a bus stop, braked to a halt, and threw the engine into neutral. Slamming on the emergency brake, he opened the door on his side.

Hutch tossed him his wallet, open to his ID. "Here! Tell 'em who we are!"

The police car had pulled into the bus stop right behind them. It was a two-man car, and a uniformed officer was emerging from either side as Starsky got out of the Torino.

Hutch's wallet in his left hand, Starsky reached for his hip pocket with his right to get out his own. Misreading his intentions, both policemen ducked behind their open doors with drawn guns.

The policeman on the driver's side yelled, "Freeze, mister!"

"We're cops, too!" Starsky yelled back. "Look!"

He slid Hutch's wallet under the open door to the driver, waited until he had picked it up and looked at it, then cautiously drew out his own. He slid it to the other policeman.

Both cops came to their feet, holstered their guns, and came around in front of the police car. Starsky ran over with both hands outstretched.

"Quick!" he said. "We're tailing a suspect!"

The police officers hurriedly handed back the wallets. The driver said apologetically, "We had no way of knowing. Sorry, Officer Hutchinson."

Starsky was racing back toward the Torino. Over his shoulder he snarled, "Dammit, I'm Starsky. *He's* Hutch!"

A city bus double-parked just behind the police car and began to blast its horn. Without glancing back, Starsky dived into the front seat of the Torino, released the emergency brake, and shot forward again.

Within half a block the Torino was doing sixty. By the end of the block the speedometer touched seventy. Hutch was again peering through the binoculars.

They roared past Western Avenue and on for another half-dozen blocks. As they neared Crenshaw Boulevard, Hutch lowered the glasses to his lap and said disgustedly, "No sign of him for a half-mile ahead. We should have spotted him by now if he was still traveling Wilshire. We've lost him again."

Slowing, then pulling over to halt in another bus stop, Starsky asked, "What now?"

"I suppose we could cruise some of the side streets off Wilshire," Hutch said with glum certainly that it was a pointless suggestion.

"Yeah," Starsky said with equal glumness. "Can't be more than twenty or thirty between here and where we lost him. Which direction off of Wilshire you suggest we cruise each street, and how far?"

"Oh, the hell with it," Hutch said. "We blew it."

Sighing, Starsky switched on the left-turn blinker and glanced into his sideview mirror before pulling out from the curb. Then a strange look suddenly formed on his face and his head swiveled back to look at his partner again.

"Something just occurred to me," he said. "Isn't Wilton Place around here somewhere?"

"Back a few blocks, this side of Western. Why?"

"I remember that the society page write-up of his engagement said Henderson lived on Wilton Place. Maybe he was going home for something before meeting the shotgun twins."

"Worth a try," Hutch said, perking up. "Let's hit it."

Again checking the traffic behind him in the sideview mirror, Starsky pulled out, saw that the street was clear of on-coming traffic at the moment, too, and made an illegal U-turn. He roared back to Wilton Place and turned right. Then he slowed to cruising speed as they drifted south for several blocks, Starsky scanning his side of the street for the green Jaguar while Hutch checked the right side.

"Sure it was south of Wilshire?" Hutch finally asked.

Starsky shook his head. "Only that it was on Wilton Place. Maybe we better try the other direction."

He made another U-turn, drove back to Wilshire Boulevard at high speed, and crossed it. On the other side he slowed to cruising speed, and again the two detectives began to scan their own sides of the street.

Hutch suddenly announced, "I spotted it!"

Chapter 21

STARSKY INSTANTLY BRAKED and pulled over to double-park. Glancing ahead, he could see no parking places clear to the next corner. In his rearview mirror he could see none behind him either.

He looked at Hutch, who was swiveled sideways to peer through the back window. Starsky checked the rearview mirror again, but could not spot the reflection of the Jaguar in it.

"I don't see it," he said.

"You can see it from here," Hutch said. "It's in one of the carports of that pink stucco apartment building a quarter of a block back. I caught a glimpse of it as we drove by."

Wilton Place was not a heavily traveled street, but there was enough traffic on it so that they could hardly remain double-parked. Starsky set the emergency brake and climbed out of the car.

"I'll check it out," he said. "You see if you can find a parking place."

Nodding, Hutch moved over into the driver's seat. Starsky slammed the car door and walked back toward the pink stucco apartment building.

It was a building of only two stories, with probably ten apartments on each floor. While a fairly new, fashionable-looking place, it wasn't in the same class with some of the more expensive apartment houses farther west, in Beverly Hills and West Los Angeles. Starsky was a little surprised, because he had been under the impression that Mark Henderson was not just well off, but rich.

A driveway perpendicular to the street ran alongside the south side of the building, and the carports were off it. Starsky walked past the front of the building to the driveway and glanced down it. The Jaguar was in the third carport back from the street.

He backtracked to the walk leading from the sidewalk to the front entrance to the apartment house and turned along it. There was a tiled lobby with stairs leading to the upper floor straight ahead, and mailboxes on each of the two side walls. Starsky checked the cards beneath the mailboxes to the right first, which seemed to be for the second-floor apartments, and immediately spotted the name *Mark Henderson*. His apartment number was 204.

Starsky went out front again. Glancing up the street, he saw the Torino backing into a parking place on the opposite side a half-block away. He walked out into the middle of the street, and as the red and white sedan finished sliding into place, he made a pushing motion with his upraised right hand, signaling Hutch to stay there. Hutch stuck his left hand out of the window, the thumb and forefinger formed into an "O" in acknowledgment of the message.

Starsky waited for a passing car, then continued across the street. There was another apartment house there whose front entrance was directly across from the driveway leading to the carports of the pink stucco building. Starsky entered its lobby and stood watching through the glass front door. From that vantage point he could see both the Jaguar and the front entrance of the apartment building across the street.

Up in apartment 204 Mark Henderson was examining himself in his bathroom mirror. Satisfied, he went into the bedroom, opened a bureau drawer and took out a small pearl-handled .25-caliber semiautomatic. Rummaging beneath a stack of handkerchiefs, he located a box of ammunition, ejected the clip, and fully loaded it. He replaced the box of ammunition where he had found it, drew back the gun's slide to put a shell in the chamber, and set the safety catch. He dropped the pistol into the right-hand side pocket of his suit coat.

He went through the front room and cracked open the door into the corridor. No one was there. He hadn't really expected to find any of his neighbors in the hallway, because most of them were working people who wouldn't be home at this time of day, but he felt the precaution was necessary to avoid having to explain his present appearance.

Slipping into the corridor, he locked the door behind him and hurried to the stairs. He met no one on the way down or in the lower lobby.

From across the street Starsky watched as a grayhaired man wearing a gray mustache, dark sunglasses, and a black Homburg came from the pink stucco apartment building and turned in the direction of the driveway leading to the carports. Starsky probably would have paid no attention to him if he hadn't been wearing a blue pin-stripe suit identical to the one Mark Henderson had been wearing when they spotted him going to lunch and when the Jaguar had driven in front of them on Wilshire Boulevard. That made him study the man closely, and he realized that his muscular body was the same size and shape as that of the assistant district attorney.

He was therefore not greatly surprised when the man walked along the driveway and got into the green Jaguar. The sports car backed out of the carport, turned his way, and drove to the street. The car turned left toward Wilshire.

Opening the door, Starsky ran outside. By the time he reached the sidewalk, the Jaguar was a block away. Hutch had seen it pull from the driveway, too, but a sudden burst of traffic going south forced him to wait while three other cars passed before he could pull away from the curb. That was probably just as well, even though it did delay pursuit, because it gave the Torino a buffer zone on the normally trafficless street in case Henderson glanced into his rearview mirror.

The Torino braked to a halt alongside Starsky, and he slid into the passenger seat. By now the Jaguar was a good two blocks ahead of them. Hutch stepped on the accelerator until he was right behind the third car that had gone by before he could pull from his parking place, then held that position.

"He's in disguise," Starsky said. "Gray hair, gray false mustache, and dark glasses. Also a black Homburg. But the same suit he was wearing."

Peering ahead, Hutch said, "He's taking a left at Wilshire. What do you suppose that's for?"

"I suppose Zale and Canelli are holed up somewhere in that direction."

"No, I mean the disguise."

"Oh. I suppose he doesn't want to take a change on being recognized anywhere around the shotgun twins."

The three cars ahead of them had all turned right at Wilshire. Hutch had to wait a few seconds before traffic cleared enough for him to make a left turn. He speeded up until they spotted the Jaguar ahead, then slowed to the same speed as the other traffic, again keeping three cars between the Torino and the car they were tailing.

"I've got another theory," Hutch said.

"About what?"

"What the hell were we talking about? The disguise."

"Oh. Want to let me in on it?"

Hutch said, "Henderson must be pretty cold-blooded to have had young Cather killed along with the girl he had gotten pregnant."

"I'll go along with that," Starsky agreed. "Suppose he figured it as a safety play against the possibility of future blackmail. Get rid of the only witness who could testify against him."

"Not the only one," Hutch said. "There's Zane and Canelli."

Starsky looked at him.

"And Fat Rolly just delivered an ultimatum to Henderson from the shotgun twins to be there in an hour or they'd blow the whistle on him. What do you suppose he thinks they want? Put yourself in his place."

Starsky continued to look at him. Finally he said slowly, "If it was me, I'd expect the boys to make some kind of blackmail demand."

"Uh-huh," Hutch agreed. "And if Henderson's capable of having a kid wiped out just on the off chance he might be a blackmail threat sometime in the dim future, how do think he's going to react to what he probably figures is going to be an open attempt to blackmail him?"

"You've got more than just a theory there," Starsky said. "It's damn near a certainty that he's in that disguise because he plans to kill both of them."

"Which makes us the avenging angels," Hutch said wryly. "Because we set it up. I doubt that Zale and Canelli will be any loss to society, but cops are supposed to protect even citizens as depraved as they are when their lives are in danger."

"Yeah," Starsky said. "I guess we better move in before he can get his licks in."

This time they didn't lose the Jaguar. It led them clear to the end of Wilshire Boulevard, left on Grand to Sixth Street, and right on Sixth, which was one-way east at that point. They passed Los Angeles Street, continued on to San Pedro Street, turned left there to Third, then left again on that one-way street going west.

The Torino barely made it to the corner of San Pedro and Third in time to see the Jaguar's rear end disappearing down the entry ramp of a basement garage on the left side of the street a half-block away. When they neared the building the garage was in, they saw it was a dilapidated hotel.

Starsky slid the rack from under the front seat, lifted out the two citizens' band radios, and tossed one on the seat next to Hutch. He slid the rack back in place. Hutch brought the Torino to a stop in front of the hotel. Starsky jumped out and ran around to the curb side.

Spotting an alley running from the street alongside the far end of the hotel, Hutch yelled after Starsky, "I'll cover the back! Let me know!"

Starsky raised the small radio in his left hand in acknowledgment as he sprinted up the steps of the hotel and into the lobby. He halted there to take a quick look around.

To the right was an unmanned registration desk with a push bell on it and a sign reading RING BELL FOR SERVICE. Directly across the dingy lobby from the front door was a single elevator. To its left was a stairway.

The floor indicator above the elevator showed that the car was on the fifth floor. But Starsky figured Henderson would not have had time as yet even to park his car in the basement garage and get over to the elevator.

Just in case Henderson intended to take the car

only as far as the lobby floor, Starsky went over to the street side of the registration desk, where he could drop out of sight the instant the elevator door started to open.

His gaze on the elevator floor indicator, he switched on the radio and said, "Hutch?"

Meantime Hutch had swung into the alley running alongside the building and had gunned the Torino to an intersecting alley running behind the hotel. He swung right, braked, then backed until he was directly opposite the hotel's rear door, but was faced so that he could barrel down the alley running into Third Street again, in case it was necessary to get back around to the front of the hotel in a hurry.

Setting the brake, but leaving the engine running, Hutch dropped his Beretta on the seat next to him and picked up the radio. He switched it on just in time to hear Starsky's voice say, "Hutch?"

"In position," Hutch said. "What's the situation?"

"Lobby's empty. Elevator indicator shows the car's on the fifth floor, but Henderson didn't take it there, because he hasn't had time. . . . Wait a minute. It just started down. Four—three—Jesus, this is a slow-moving elevator. Must date back to World War I. Two—one—it's passed one and is going to the basement. That has to be Henderson."

"Are there stairs?" Hutch asked.

"City fire code requires it."

"Do you know where the hell they are?" Hutch asked patiently.

"Sure, right across the lobby from me. Slow as this elevator moves, I ought to be able to keep up with it—'B' just blinked out on the indicator. He's coming up."

Chapter 22

As STARSKY WATCHED, the number "1" lighted up on the floor indicator. He was prepared to drop below the desk top if the door started to open, but the number blinked out again, indicating that the car was rising to at least the second floor.

Charging across the lobby, he said into the radio, "Elevator's heading up! I'm taking the stairs."

He went up the stairs three at a time. At the second floor he paused long enough to look across the hallway at the floor indicator. He had beaten the elevator by several seconds; as he watched, the number "2" blinked on, then off again.

Barking into the radio, "Heading for third," he raced up the next flight.

He reached the third floor just in time to see the number "3" blink on and off again. This time he had only tied the speed of the elevator.

"Heading for fourth," he said into the radio, continuing his race upward.

"Hang in there," Hutch's voice came from the radio. "I think there's only nine stories."

Starsky was breathing heavily when he reached four. He was just in time to see the number "4" blink off.

As he started to race upward again, he gasped into

the radio, "On to fifth. Remember how I said it was a toilet?"

"Yeah," Hutch's voice came back.

"Well, somebody up there is flushing!"

When Starsky reached the fifth floor, no indicator light was showing, but since the elevator door was closed, he knew the car had gone beyond there. He also knew that at that rate he was losing ground. If the car rose more than another two stories, he wasn't going to catch up to it until long after Henderson had gotten off, if he managed to catch up with it at all.

"Heading for sixth," he croaked into the radio, forcing himself to continue on upward, but now moving at a lumbering stagger. He tried to increase his upward momentum by grabbing the handrail each time he took another step, and pulling himself along.

On the landing between the fifth and sixth floors a teen-age boy and girl were entwined in each other's arms, passionately kissing. Starsky's feet, sponge-soled, were making no appreciable noise on the stairway, but they must have heard his wheezing breath, because they split apart and looked at him just as he got there. Plunging between them, wheezing like an asthmatic, he blundered on.

At the sixth floor there was no indicator light showing either, but as he momentarily halted, number "7" went on.

"Heading for seventh," he croaked into the radio, and staggered on upward.

"Lucky number, man," Hutch's voice came back. "Hang on as long as you're faded."

Starsky gave out just before he reached the seventh floor. He collapsed to his hands and knees, his palms resting on the second step from the top, his knees hitting the fourth one from the top. There was no way he could even crawl another inch. His breath went in and out in great whooping gasps.

The position into which he had collapsed put his head just above floor level. Through a red haze he could see that the number "7" was still lit on the floor indicator and that the elevator door was open.

When he shook his head, the red haze lifted, but his tortured lungs still drew in and expelled air in huge gasps. And there was no way he could have gotten to his feet.

At the far end of the hall, fortunately too far away to hear the anguished sound of Starsky's breathing, the detective spotted Mark Henderson standing before a door, looking at the number. As he watched, the assistant district attorney took a small semiautomatic from his pocket, checked it, and put it away again. He raised his fist to knock on the door.

Starsky's mind told him to run down the hallway with drawn gun covering Henderson, order the man to freeze before he could knock on that door, and handcuff him. It was his duty to prevent him from murdering the two men in that room.

But Starsky had no strength left. It took supreme effort for him to summon even enough energy to turn around and sit on the fourth step down, instead of remaining in his kneeling position. That put his head below floor level, out of Henderson's sight if he had happened to glance that way. Starsky sat there wheezing, unable to move, unable to speak into the radio, unable to do anything but fill his tortured lungs with deep gulps of air and expel again.

The radio said, "What's happening, Starsk? Come in, will you? What's going on?"

Starsky merely sat there wheezing.

When Mark Henderson knocked on the door at the other end of the hallway, there was no response for perhaps half a minute. But the assistant D.A. had the feeling he was being examined through the little peephole in the door.

Finally a muffled voice called from the other side of the door, "Who is it?"

"You knew perfectly well who it is," Henderson said testily. "It's Henderson."

There was the sound of a lock turning, and the door opened. The thin, hook-nosed Canelli stood in the doorway in his undershirt. Beyond him, seated on the bed with his shoes off, looking toward the door, Henderson could see the pale, squarely built Zale. Canelli stepped aside and Henderson moved into the room, fingering the gun in the side pocket of his suit coat.

"How the hell am I supposed to know perfectly well who it is in that outfit?" Canelli asked. "Why the get-up?"

"I can't afford to be seen visiting you gentlemen."

Henderson examined both men carefully. Neither seemed to be armed. Right now was the time to do it, he thought. It would have to be sudden and unexpected, because they were as dangerous as a pair of rattlesnakes. Hesitation could be fatal.

But he was not a practiced killer, even though it hadn't troubled his conscience in the least to order two other people killed. There is a difference between long-distance killing and face-to-face killing. It takes a different kind of guts for an infantryman to thrust a bayonet into an enemy soldier than it does for an artilleryman to pull the lanyard of a cannon ten miles behind the lines, even though the cannon fire may kill a hundred enemies. Henderson realized it was going to take supreme effort to force himself to draw the gun and start shooting.

Zale said in an admiring tone, "Hey, that's a pretty good makeup job. Where'd you get the talent, Counselor?"

"I've been involved in Little Theater," Henderson said a trifle woodenly. "Just what is this urgent matter that required my presence within the hour?"

"What urgent matter?" Canelli asked.

"That's what I asked you." Henderson's hand closed about the gun in his pocket, and his finger slipped under the trigger guard. "The message you had Fat Rolly phone me."

"We didn't have Fat Rolly phone you nothing," Canelli said. "What in hell you talking about?"

Henderson frowned at him without understanding. "It was Rolly's voice. In fact there's no question about it being Rolly. You didn't have him call me at my office a while ago to deliver your ultimatum?"

"What ultimatum?" Zale inquired.

"That if I were not here within one hour, you would phone the police. I believe the way Rolly put it was that you would blow the whistle."

Canelli and Zale exchanged frowning glances. "What's that tub of lard trying to pull?" Zale asked. "We ain't even seen him since yesterday."

Henderson's gaze flicked from one man to the other. The puzzled looks on their faces made it obvious they were telling the truth. Taking his hand from his coat pocket, he went over to the phone on the dresser.

"There's never no one on the switchboard," Canelli said. "You got to dial eight for an outside line."

Nodding, Henderson dialed a number. It rang several times before a gruff male voice answered, "Fat Rolly's Bargain Circus."

"Rolly, please," Henderson said.

"Ain't here."

"Can you tell me how to get in touch with him?"

"Who's calling?" the gruff voice asked.

"A friend. This is quite urgent."

"Well, friend, when you think of your name, call back."

The phone clicked. Taking it from his ear, Henderson gazed at Canelli and Zale in astonishment.

"He hung up on me," he said with outraged indignation.

The heavy-set Zale got up from the bed and took the phone from Henderson's hand. "Dial it again," he said.

Henderson dialed the number, then bent his head next to Zale's to listen to the conversation. Canelli came over to stand on the other side of his partner and listen, too.

The same gruff voice again answered, "Fat Rolly's Bargain Circus."

Zale growled into the phone, "Who's this?"

"Who are you?" the gruff voice countered.

"Zale."

The man's tone instantly changed. "Oh, yes, Mr. Zale," he said respectfully. "Sorry I didn't recognize your voice. This is Leo."

"Lemme talk to Rolly, Leo," Zale said.

"He ain't here, Mr. Zale. Somebody else just called for him, too."

"I know," Zale said. "Where is Rolly?"

"He got busted."

"Busted for what?"

"I ain't sure. Marty and me wasn't either one of us here when they led him off. We was taking a walk about a block away when we seen these two cops go by with Rolly in the back seat. Way he was sittin', looked like they had his hands cuffed behind him, so I'm pretty sure it was a bust."

"You don't have any idea what it was about?" Zale asked.

"Well, before Marty and me left, the cops was talking to Rolly about a lot of stuff. First they accused him of spreading a story that got Manny Torro scratched. You hear about that?"

"No, but the hell with Manny Torro," Zale said

impatiently. "What else were the cops leaning on him about?"

"They mentioned you and Mr. Canelli."

"What about us?" Zale asked in a sharp tone.

"I don't know what it was about. One of the cops told Rolly he was taking a risk getting involved with people like you and Canelli. Rolly said he never heard of you. Then the other cop said something about Rolly running errands for Assistant District Attorney Mark Henderson. Rolly said he never heard of him either."

Mark Henderson drew in an audible breath. Zale growled, "Who was these cops, Leo?"

"Couple of detectives named Starsky and Hutchinson."

For a frozen instant Zale, Canelli, and Henderson all stopped breathing. Then Zale hung up, ran over to seat himself on the bed, and hurriedly began to put on his shoes. Canelli ran to the clothes closet, whipped a shirt from a coat hanger, and put it on.

"You dummy!" Canelli snarled at Henderson. "You let them set you up. If the outside is crawling with cops, you're going out first as a shield."

Paling, Henderson threw a fearful look at the closed door.

Chapter 23

CANELLI JERKED TWO jackets from hangers in the closet, threw one onto the bed next to his partner, and slipped into the other. Then he reached to the closet floor, lifted out the two black leather shotgun cases, and tossed one onto the bed on the other side of his partner. Canelli set his case down on the scarred dresser top, took the sawed-off shotgun from it, and broke it to examine the load. Zale, his shoes and jacket both now on, was doing the same thing on the bed.

Canelli snapped the shotgun closed, lay it on the dresser top, and jerked open a dresser drawer. Pulling out two .45-caliber Colt automatics, he called, "Heads up!" to Zale, and tossed him one.

Expertly catching it by the butt, Zale drew back the slide just far enough to make sure a shell was in the chamber, let it snap forward again, set the safety, and tucked the gun into his belt beneath his jacket. After checking his and setting the safety, Canelli thrust it into a hip pocket.

Both men picked up their shotguns. Canelli went over to peer out of the seventh-story window down into the alley. Zale went over to look through the peephole into the hallway.

"That goddamned Torino of Starsky's is parked out back," Canelli announced.

Henderson, his face now dead white, went over to look out of the window, too.

"Take a good look, you capon shyster!" Canelli snarled at him. "You let them sucker you into leading them right to us!"

Henderson said in a shaking voice, "They can't have any proof. They're just fishing. Let's not do anything rash. I can beat this in court for all of us."

"Beat it for yourself, stupid!" Canelli snapped. "We're busting out of here. Ready, Zale?"

Zale, his eye still to the peephole, said, "There's nobody in the hall. Maybe they only followed him to the hotel, and don't know what room we're in. If they're making a floor-to-floor search, it could be a hell of a long time before they got up here. Might give us enough time."

"To do what?" Canelli asked.

"Make the roof. It's only about a four-foot jump to the flophouse next door, and we could take the fire escape down from it. Worth a chance."

"Well, let's get moving then," Canelli said, starting for the door.

"May I go with you?" Henderson asked in a high voice.

Without looking around, Canelli growled, "Suit yourself, buster."

Hutch's increasingly worried voice made repeated inquiries over the radio before Starsky finally regained sufficient breath to answer. Even then he had to speak haltingly, between heavily indrawn breaths and equally heavy expulsions of air.

"I'm—on—the—seventh—floor—Hutch. This—was—end—of—line."

"You sound like you've been running, Starsk. Why the long silence?"

"Recovering—my breath," Starsky said, this time managing to get two words in between respirations. Then his improvement was rapid. "I spotted the—room. Hang on."

Gripping the handrail in order to pull himself to his feet, he turned and cautiously poked his head around the edge of the stairwell. Into the radio he said, "Door's closed, Henderson's not in sight, and the elevator car's still on this floor. My deduction is that he's in the room."

"How do you do it, Mr. Holmes?" Hutch asked admiringly.

Ignoring the sarcasm, Starsky said, "I don't think we need you covering the rear any more. They're pretty well boxed."

"Want me to come up there?" Hutch asked.

"No. Let's use a little psychological warfare. When I give you the signal, you make like a million cops surrounding the hotel."

"How do you make like a million cops?" Hutch inquired interestedly.

"With your siren and wailer. Those two little buttons on the dashboard. One makes a siren noise like a fire engine, the other a wail like a banshee."

"You're getting funnier by the day," Hutch said. "But you could use a new writer. You think psychology will work on a pair like Canelli and Zane?"

"They're pros, Hutch. I figure they'll play the odds. If they think they haven't got a chance, they just might throw out their guns."

"Okay, we'll play it that way," Hutch said. "But be careful. Those sawed-off shotguns make big holes."

"I'm always careful," Starsky said. "You ready to go into action?"

"All set," Hutch's voice said from the radio.

Hearing a giggle from down below, Starsky drew back and peered over the railing. The two teen-agers were still on the landing a flight and a half below. The boy now had her seated on the steps and was on his knees on the landing facing her, trying to force her knees apart.

Starsky continued to gaze downward, fascinated for a moment, then tore his attention away and peered around the edge of the stairwell again. The corridor was still deserted. Drawing his .38, he walked quickly but quietly along the hall toward the door where he had seen Mark Henderson.

As he neared the door, he saw that its number was 717. Simultaneously he saw that the door at the very end of the dead-end hallway, facing him and only about twenty feet beyond room 717, was slightly ajar.

His reaction was instinctive. Knowing that if a gun were aimed at him from the doorway, his only hope was unexpected offense, he lowered his head and charged the twenty feet like an offensive fullback hitting the opposing line. The door smashed inward, he fell into a crouch in the center of the room, and spun in a complete circle to cover all corners of the room with his gun.

The room was not only empty, it had an unused look, as though it had not been occupied for some time. It was just a tenantless room, Starsky realized, and the maid had neglected to lock it after putting it in shape for the next tenant.

Feeling a little silly, he returned to room 717 and put his ear to the door.

"May I go with you?" he heard Mark Henderson ask in a strangely high voice. Then another, gruffer voice said, "Suit yourself, buster."

Apparently Henderson hadn't started murdering anyone yet, Starsky thought with relief. Reaching out, he pounded his knuckles against the door and called out,

"All right in there! This is the police! Open up!"

Instantly stepping to one side of the door, he said into the radio with urgency, "NOW—NOW—NOW!"

Down behind the hotel Hutch hit the siren and the gas at the same time. As the siren began to scream, Hutch sent the Torino around the corner into the alley leading to Third Street, and roared along it to make a sharp left turn onto Third. He threw the car into reverse and screeched backward past the down ramp into the basement garage, coming to a halt directly in front of the hotel. He cut the siren button and hit the wailer button. Heads began popping from windows, and people began emerging from buildings all along the street.

Up on the seventh floor Starsky could hear both the siren and the wailer. Into the radio he said, "Sounds like a million cops. Good act."

Then, adding his own voice to the furor, Starsky called, "Open up in there or we're all coming in!"

There was a blast like a grenade exploding in a rain barrel, and the center part of the door disintegrated, leaving a hole big enough for a man to run through at a crouch. From the sound of the explosion Starsky judged that only one barrel of one shotgun had been discharged, but the damage rendered by that single shot convinced him beyond doubt that the ammunition being used was what he had previously suspected: magnum shells loaded with 00 shot.

Starsky backtracked rapidly through the open door of the room at the end of the hall, his .38 leveled at the gaping hole in the door. Canelli shot through the hole crouched over, his still-smoking shotgun swinging toward Starsky.

Starsky started to say, "Freeze!" changed his mind as he saw the man's finger begin to whiten on the trigger, and instead threw himself to one side of the door just as the second barrel of the shotgun went off.

Across the room behind Starsky the entire window blew out into the alley that ran alongside the hotel. Starsky scrambled to a prone position in the doorway just in time to see Canelli running for the elevator, and Zale rushing in a crouch through the gaping hole in the door. As Zale's shotgun swung toward him, Starsky rolled aside again only an instant before the gun blasted. This time hunks of plaster showered down from the wall alongside the window behind Starsky.

Starsky rolled back into the doorway again to see Zale racing for the elevator. Canelli, no longer in sight, presumably was already on it.

As Starsky leveled his gun at Zale, Mark Henderson ran into the hallway, bent over, and straightened up with his hands raised.

"Wait!" he called after Zale. "Don't run! They haven't got—"

"Get out of the way!" Starsky yelled at him. "Move!"

Zale swung around, and the second barrel of his shotgun blasted. Henderson, directly between the gun and Starsky, took the full charge. He was driven backward, landing on his back and skidding along the floor. His body, unrecognizable because it lacked a face and had very little head left, came to rest only a few feet in front of the prone detective.

Starsky got off one shot as Zale ducked into the elevator, but it missed. The elevator door closed.

Chapter 24

THE SHOTGUN BLASTS were so loud that Hutch heard them clear down the street, seven stories below, even above the undulating scream of the wailer. He instantly cut the wailer so that his voice could be heard on the radio.

"Starsk?" he asked anxiously.

In a breathless voice indicating he was running, Starsky said, "Henderson's dead, and Canelli and Zale are in the elevator, heading down. Lobby or parking garage."

Since he was parked on the left side of the one-way street, Hutch was seated behind the wheel on the curb side. He scrambled out the other door, scooping up his Beretta en route.

A considerable crowd had now gathered on both sides of the street, brought outdoors by the screaming wailer. At the top of his voice Hutch yelled, "Get under cover, folks! There's going to be shooting!"

One of the rubberneckers was an elderly man, presumably the usually invisible hotel desk clerk, who had come from the hotel's front door and was standing at the top of the steps looking down. He scurried back inside.

Hutch leaned across the hood of the Torino, his Beretta aimed at the front door of the hotel, his gun hand steadied by gripping the wrist with his left hand. All around him he could hear people scurrying to get out of the line of fire.

On the seventh floor Starsky had avoided looking down at the shattered body of Mark Henderson as he stepped over it. He had been halfway along the hall to the stairs when Hutch's voice had come over the radio. By the time their brief exchange was over, he was at the stairway.

Until he reached the stairs, Starsky had merely been reacting instinctively, but as he started down, it hit him that he was going to have to descend seven stories, or fourteen flights of stairs. The thought caught him in the stomach like a blow to the solar plexus. By now he had fully recovered his breath from the fourteen-flight climb, but he had by no means recovered his stamina. He was on the verge of physical exhaustion.

"Merciful mother!" he said aloud as he started the downward trip.

At each floor the stairway reversed direction. As he pivoted around the stair post at six without slowing down, he glanced at the elevator indicator across the hall. It registered "5," which meant the elevator had one full floor's lead on him.

He went down the next flight like a demented mountain goat, vaulting the two astonished teen-agers, now prone on the steps, staggering when he hit flat-footed on the landing just beyond them, but recovering and hurtling on.

His descent from there on was more of a controlled fall than anything else. He was so exhausted that he was afraid he would collapse in a heap if he slowed even for an instant. He kept hurtling along with the same unreasoning conviction that speed was vital to his getting there at all, like a motorist reasons when he speeds to get to a gas station before he runs out of gas. He let gravity take him down, preserving what energy he had left for navigation. That was difficult, too, because he couldn't grip the handrails to steady himself; his pistol was in one hand and the radio in the other. Whenever he started to lose balance, which was often, he righted himself by throwing a hip against the railing on one side or the other, and sort of sliding along the railing until he could recover.

At the fifth floor no number was showing on the elevator indicator, and he didn't wait to see what was going to blink on. But at the next floor the number "4" was lighted as he pivoted around the turn. He had caught up with the descending car.

When he hurtled around the turn in the stairway a three, again no light was showing, but as he reached the second floor, the number "3" light blinked on. He was now a floor ahead.

When he got to the lobby, gasping for breath, the indicator showed no number. He staggered across the lobby to the registration desk and propped himself against its far side to keep himself from falling, his gun aimed in the direction of the elevator, but wavering so badly that he wondered if he could even hit the door when and if it opened, let alone the two gunmen on the car.

Through an open door behind the desk to his right he became conscious of an elderly man peering out at him fearfully.

The number "1" blinked on above the elevator door, and he attempted to steady his gun. Then it blinked off again without the door opening, which meant the pair was heading for the basement.

"Oh, my God!" Starsky said aloud, suddenly realizing he didn't know where the stairs to the basement were. The stairway he had just descended ended at the lobby, and no other stairs were in evidence. He assumed the ones to the basement were somewhere along the hallway leading from the lobby to the rear door, but there was no time for exploration.

From some untapped and unrealized reserve he summoned the energy to race to the front door and outside. Hutch was leaning over the hood of the Torino, his gun aimed at Starsky.

"Parking garage!" Starsky croaked as he rushed down the outside steps.

Hutch instantly straightened, jerked open the car's right-hand door, and threw himself across the seat and under the steering wheel. The engine was already running, so all he had to do was release the brake, shift, and slam down the accelerator. The Torino leaped forward, he swung in a squealing left turn, and was roaring down the entry ramp into the underground garage before Starsky could get halfway to it on foot.

As he reached the bottom of the ramp, Hutch spotted the elevator door off to his left and gunned the car directly at it. The door began to open as he neared.

Zale and Canelli started to hurry from the car, then saw the Torino racing toward them, apparently intent on driving right through the open elevator door to crash into the elevator's rear wall. Abruptly changing their minds, the two gunmen threw themselves on either side of the door inside the elevator.

At the last instant Hutch hit the brakes hard, cramped the wheel sharply to the right, and skidded the car sideways to come to rest within a foot of the open elevator door, trapping the two gunmen inside.

Slipping into neutral and slamming on the emergency brake, Hutch tumbled out the right-hand door and ran in a crouch for cover behind one of the thick concrete support pillars.

Starsky came loping down the entry ramp, took in the situation at a glance, and dived for cover behind a car parked just at the foot of the ramp. Panting for breath, he looked around for Hutch.

He located him when Hutch called from behind a nearby pillar, "Police! You're wired! Throw out your guns and give it up!"

Two sawed-off shotguns came flying across the hood to clatter onto the concrete floor. Hutch stood and stepped from behind the pillar, his Beretta aimed at the elevator door.

"Watch it, Hutch!" Starsky called. "Those shotguns were empty anyway. They may have other guns."

The powerfully built Zale suddenly dived across the hood of the Torino and landed on his hands and knees the other side of it. Dropping prone, he fired his Colt automatic at Hutch. The slug chipped concrete from the pillar alongside the detective's head.

Popping up from behind the hood of the car where he had taken cover, Starsky squeezed off four shots so rapidly that they seemed to run together into one continuous explosion. Zale's body jerked as though he were having an epileptic fit.

Canelli threw himself across the Torino's hood, and his .45 automatic roared five times. Starsky ducked under cover just before the first shot and heard all five slugs whistle over his head where he had been standing an instant before.

Then Hutch's Baretta chattered. When it stopped, Starsky raised his head for a cautious look over the hood. Canelli was collapsed across the hood of the Torino, his right arm hanging downward on one side of it. The gun slipped from his lifeless fingers as Starsky watched, clanking onto the concrete floor.

Starsky and Hutch both cautiously approached the fallen gunmen. Zale, face down on the concrete floor, didn't move, but still clutched his pistol in his outstretched hand. Hutch moved in on him from the side and kicked the weapon away.

The two detectives put away their guns. Looking at each other, both sighed. Their faces were suddenly old, not with years, but with bitter experience.

Hutch went over to the Torino. "I'll call in," he said.

Nodding, Starsky began to collect the weapons lying on the floor.

Huggy Bear's was crowded with dinner trade when Starsky and Hutch entered the café. Huggy Bear himself was on duty behind the bar, resplendent in a red and white checkered shirt and a blue bow tie.

He said, "It was on TV that you boys were in a pretty bad shoot-em-up this afternoon."

"Yeah," Starsky said in a depressed tone. "Booth going to be available any time soon?"

"Forty-five minutes," the black man said. "There's a waiting list."

Starsky said to Hutch, "I got a date with Cindy at eight. Let's sit at the bar."

Shrugging, Hutch slipped onto a vacant bar stool. Starsky sat next to him.

"Some chick left a message for you, Hutch," Huggy Bear said. "Called long-distance from Chicago."

"Who?"

"Somebody named Molly. Said she'd be in on the midnight flight. If you're interested, you're supposed to phone the airport and leave a message. And leave the key in the usual place."

"Well, well," Hutch said. "You didn't wreck the relationship after all, Starsk."

"You mean I didn't save you from a fate worse than death," Starsky said cynically. "She must be after you. I'll be best man at the wedding."

"That'll be the day," Hutch told him.

They both ordered, Hutch choosing from Angie the chef's limited menu of health foods, Starsky ordering a steak. After placing their orders, Starsky went over to the candy machine near the door and dropped in a quarter. He made a selection and pulled the lever. Nothing came out.

He made an alternate selection and pulled that lever. Still no candy bar dropped into the slot. He kicked the machine.

"Hey!" Huggy Bear called. "That machine cost money."

"You don't understand the psychology of machines," Hutch said, getting up and going over to it.

He pulled a lever at random, and a candy bar dropped into the slot. Picking it up, Starsky examined it and made a face.

"I don't like that kind," he complained. Stopping a passing waiter, he handed it to him. "Here."

The waiter looked vaguely surprised, but he accepted the bar, dropped it into his pocket, and said, "Thanks."

Starsky produced another quarter and dropped it into the machine. He pulled the same lever he had previously selected as first choice. Nothing happened. He made the same alternate choice as before, and again no candy bar dropped. He kicked the machine again.

"Hey, cut that out!" Huggy Bear called.

Hutch started to reach for a lever, but Starsky slapped his hand. "Your choices are awful," he said.

He tried the same two levers again, then tried two more. When no candy dropped, he gave up in disgust.

"The hell with it," he said, returning to the bar.

Hutch resumed his seat also. "You're better off anyway," he said. "That stuff rots your teeth, eats your stomach, and makes you fat."

The front door opened and two young, attractive black women came in together. Just as they started past the candy machine, it made a whirring noise and disgorged a bar of candy. The girls stopped to look, then one reached to lift the candy from the slot.

Starsky started to get up from his stool, but before he could say anything, the girl had stripped off the wrapper and taken a bite. As the two girls went by toward the far end of the bar, his gaze followed the candy bar.

Climbing back on his stool, he said to Hutch, "Chocolate and nuts. My favorite kind."

"You should have lived in the Middle Ages," Hutch said. "You don't understand machines."

Bedside.
Beachside.
All around the town

▼ **Available at your local bookstore or mail the coupon below** ▼